Adventures
of Piffels
the Elf

A Fairy Tale
for Our Times

David J. Babulski

New Gaia Press
an imprint of Andborough Publishing, LLC

New Gaia Press
www.NewGaiaPress.com
Mount Airy, North Carolina 27030
USA

Cover art work: Timothy Babulski
Illustrations: David Babulski and Timothy Babulski
Cover design and book layout: Robert Yarborough

New Gaia Press is an imprint of Andborough Publishing, LLC
www.Andborough.com

Printed in the United States of America

Dedication

This story is dedicated to Gemma, without whom this project would never have been born, and to the young at heart everywhere who dare to dream.

To: Joy and Bill,
May puppets adventure be
your adventure.
David J Babulan

Table of Contents

Acknowledgments

I would like to thank Mary Belmore for her help in proofing the manuscript and my wife Karen and my son Timothy for their help in making this project a reality.

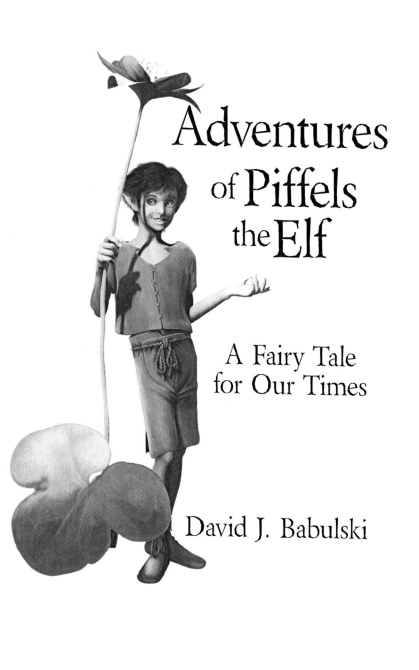

Adventures
of Piffels
the Elf

A Fairy Tale
for Our Times

David J. Babulski

Introduction

In this modern age, it is now commonplace to see elves, with their pointed ears, walking in peace and friendship with humankind and their rounded ears. This was not always the case. There was a time in the not too distant past where such friendship was unthinkable. In a desire to learn how this all came to be, you find yourself at the door of a rustic cottage set back in the woods; the home of Brave Heart Roseblossum, an elderly elf who is well known in this area as a sage of sorts. After knocking on the door, it opens and there stands an elderly elfin gentleman in a long red robe sporting an unruly white mane and full beard.

"How good of you to come; please do come in and make yourself comfortable" says the elderly elf. He moves with a fluid grace that belies his seemingly advanced age. You are ushered in to a small wood paneled room with two large chairs and a small table positioned in front of a fireplace. A small fire in the fireplace lends a cozy warmth and flickering light to the room. Rather plain and rustic in appearance, the room has warmth and charm that instantly puts you at ease. The old man sits back in his chair and puffs on a long white pipe filled with an herbal blend. A light hazy gray halo of smoke surrounds his head.

"I understand you wish to know how it all began?" asks the elderly gentleman. "Well that is a long and fascinating story." He then opens a large book resting on the small table.

"Lets see hmm, ah yes here it is." He points to a section in the book and begins to read. "It had been almost five millennia since the great conflict that tore apart the world. No longer did humankind and elf walk as brothers in love and joy. Humankind greed and elfin avarice filled hearts with hatred and distrust. Many in the humankind world desired the technology of the elves and many elves desired humankind gold and jewels. To eliminate any further conflict and loss of lives; Elves and their Fairy brethren decided to separate from the humankind world. Elfin technology was employed to reduce their size and shield them from the larger humankind world. As the centuries rolled on knowledge of the elves deteriorated into myth and myth became legend. The technology of the elves was lost to the dust of time. However, before all knowledge was lost, elfin scholars foresaw a time when one of their number, the Latra Kree, would begin the reunification of the humankind and elfin worlds. In time even the Latra Kree became a legend as the centuries rolled on. But one day an unlikely elf set in motion events that would forever change the world."

The elderly elf takes a book from the shelf and places it in your hands. "You dear friend now hold in your hands the answers to all your questions. It all begins with Chapter one. Enjoy the adventure…"

Chapter One

Hello, My Name is Piffels

It was colder than usual this morning in the observatory on Gobstop Hill as Piffels went about his morning observational duties. As it is the highest point in the elfin village of Greenbrier, Gobstop Hill was the perfect place for the Daemon's observatory. Piffels wrapped his little brown coat around his shoulders and pulled his little knit cap over his pointy ears to try and keep warm. He had observed and recorded the angle of the rising sun and noted readings from the various observatory instruments and made all the other routine observations that were required to understand the turning of the natural world. Piffels loved the natural world and was fascinated by everything from acorns to rocks, which was highly unusual for an elf. For elves, as a rule, were rather laid back little creatures and generally accepted the world as they saw it.

To most elves, being overly curious was looked upon with a great deal of suspicion. Piffels was particularly fascinated and curious about the world of humankind. Standing in the center of the hilltop observatory he now turned the great seeing glass toward the world outside the protective stonewalls and the shield of fairy glamour. The great seeing glass was a unique elf invention in that it allowed an observer to peer through the shimmer of the protective glamour shield and see the outside world. Piffels was fascinated by the many wonders of the humankind world. Of particular interest and fascination was the little girl in the back upstairs window of the humankind house in whose back gardens the elfin village of Greenbrier was located. He carefully recorded all his observations about her in his notebook. Among other things, he noted that humankind looked a lot like elves except that elves were much smaller, being about the size of half a human hand. Elves also had slightly darker skin color, and humankind had rounded ears, whereas elfin ears were slim and pointy. Humankind wore different style clothing and used very little ornamentation in their hair.

Observations were also made of the older humankind, who came and went and also lived in the house. Now as elves go, Piffels was not all that remarkable. He was small even by elfin standards, and a wee bit pudgy in the middle as was typical for most young elves. Like all elves he had slender pointy ears, light brown skin and a mop of black hair on his head that accentuated his deep blue eyes. Piffels was a stickler for precision and all his notes were neatly printed with carefully drawn illustrations of his observations. He had quite a collection of these notebooks, built up over years of observations. They were all stored in a secret compartment in one of the observatory records cupboards. Such observations of the humankind world were forbidden by elfin common law. Master Evergreen was very clear about the penalties for violation of the common law. Even so, Piffels' curiosity drove him to continue his observations. For several years he had deviated from the prescribed order of observation to observe the world of humankind and this fascinating human woman child. From his observations he deduced that she was probably about his own age of twelve years, and, like himself, was very much a dreamer and loved to go on adventures of the imagination. Like himself, she appeared to be somewhat different than the other humankind children he had observed. This humankind house stood by itself in the country with no other houses for quite some distance.

On this morning he tugged on his jacket, stood up real straight, and vowed to himself that no matter what Master Evergreen said about keeping separate from the humankind world, he would invite her into his elfin world anyway. Piffels was nothing if not a stubborn little elf.

"Plans must be made – much to do, much to do," Piffels said out loud as he began to put away all the observatory things for the morning. "Yes indeed, much to do!"

ooooo

It was a bright sunny morning with a few puffy white clouds in an otherwise bright blue sky. The two story white house stood all by itself on the little dirt road called Lollybump Drive, surrounded by tall green trees, a large back garden rich with flowers, and all manner of green growing things. It was not a very unusual sunny summer morning, but then sometimes things are not all what they seem.

"Esmeralda, Esmeralda, it is time to get up now," said Jane Hathaway as she opened the bedroom door.

"Yes, Mom." Stretching and throwing back the coverlet, Esmeralda Hathaway sat up in her bed and yawned. It was colder than usual in her bedroom this morning. The sun was streaming into the window and dust motes dancing in the sunbeams fascinated her. Walking over to the window, she opened it and smelled the fresh country air. Birds were singing and she could hear the rooster crowing in the new morning. As she looked out over the back garden with its flowers she thought to herself, "I wonder if the fairies and elves that Granny told me about live in our garden. I wonder." Breathing in the fresh air and feeling warmed by the morning sun made her feel very good inside. She said aloud, "This will be a very special day, very special indeed." Little did Esmeralda know just how special it would be!

"I'll be right down Mom," she shouted out the door as she reached into her closet for a pretty sundress. Barefoot she ran out the door and down the stairs to help her mother with breakfast. It was her favorite this morning, scrambled eggs and toast with yummy strawberry jam.

"Where is Granny this morning?" Esmeralda asked between bites of toast.

"She is out in the garden again this morning," said her mother as she wiped her hands on her apron and sat down to eat breakfast with her daughter. Granny was Esmeralda's pet name for her grandmother Beverly who lived in the house with them. Beverly Oginski was her name. She had lost her husband several years before Esmeralda was born. Beverly had come to live with her daughter Jane Hathaway and help raise little Esmeralda after her father was killed in a tragic automobile accident when Esmeralda was only six months old. The two women helped each other a great deal. Jane worked as a secretary in the adjoining town, and her mother was there to see Esmeralda off to school and to welcome her home in the afternoon. For the most part, everyone was happy. One source of friction, however, was always the older woman's devotion to the "Old Ways" of fairies, elves and magic. Jane would have none of this old ways nonsense and forbade her mother from speaking of such nonsense to Esmeralda. Which, of course she did anyway! Many were the long afternoons that Esmeralda spent at Granny's knee learning about herbs and magical stones, and listening to fascinating stories about the fairies and elves.

"I'm going to go outside and play in the back yard," said Esmeralda as she put her breakfast dish in the kitchen sink and started for the back door.

"Ok dear, have fun and be careful," said Jane. The back yard was Esmeralda's special place. A tall wooden fence surrounded the property. A large portion of the space was grass, with the back portion both a vegetable and flower garden. The gardens were Grandmother Beverly's pride and joy and Esmeralda loved to play among the flowers. One area at the very back had a special stone fence surrounding it. Esmeralda was told to never play in that place, as that was special to the fairies and elves and they did not like to be disturbed. She spent many hours peering over the rock walls, but could never see anything that looked like what she thought a fairy or elf would look like; just lots of strange looking stones and pretty flowers. But today was a beautiful summer day and she was having fun chasing butterflies.

It was a bright sunny day in the little elfin town of Greenbrier. The dirt streets were bustling with activity. At the center of Greenbrier Town was an open-air market called the Greenbrier Emporium, where merchants sold all variety of merchandise. Piffels had been sent out this morning with a small bag of exchange stones to purchase four weight of thistle down, a bag of pumpkin seed and a pouch of fairy spice for Esmenia. As he walked down the road toward the market, he thought about his life with Master Evergreen and Esmenia. The kindly old man was like a second father and he felt a great deal of fondness for him. Esmenia, the housekeeper, was kindly in her own unique brusque way, and Piffels chuckled at the thought of her sometimes strange ways.

But on this morning his thoughts drifted back to his family. Piffels was the smallest of twelve bobbins (as elf children were known). He did not quite fit with the rest of elfin society. Piffels was fascinated by the natural world and had extensive collections of pollen, rocks and stones, pressed flower petals, and other odd and unusual things of this world of the elves. It was the practice in the elfin world to apprentice children to masters of the various elfin crafts, such as weaving, farming, carpentry and so on. Piffels did not fit in one of the usual craft categories, so it was decided that he would be apprenticed to Master Evergreen the Daemon. The Daemon was the most revered of the elder elves. Each elfin village had a Daemon and it was he who told the elves when to plant and when to harvest, warned of impending danger, and in general interpreted the happenings in the natural world. Piffels missed his family so very much. Although Piffels was small and somewhat frail, he was unusually curious and bright, so Master Evergreen took him in as he had no children of his own. He loved Piffels as he would his own son. He saw great promise in this small, frail looking elf, and was training him in the ways of the Daemon, the Elen Istar. Esmenia tolerated his presence, but disliked the messes he left behind and his being underfoot all the time.

Those who were different were looked upon with a great deal of suspicion by most in elfin society. A minority of elves admired those differences, and among them Piffels counted many as dear friends. Then there were those few elves that bred fear and hatred within Piffels' little heart.

"Hey look, it's the little pet of the old fraud Evergreen," said Raggles. He and his pals, Snorf and Snaggles, loved to torment Piffels. After all, he was small and very different, and as such they felt he was little less than the dirt beneath their feet.

"Watcha doing out in the daylight, ya little freak?" said Snaggles with a sneer in his voice.

Piffels swallowed his anger at the insult, lowered his head, and walked a little faster toward town. It wasn't really worth fighting, as much as he disliked Raggles and his bunch. He tried that once and ended up bloodied and in bed for a week.

"Keep going, ya little glomsquach" said Snorf as he kicked dirt in Piffels' direction. The rest of the trip to the market went quietly, and the warm sun on his back mellowed his mood a bit. But still, Piffels kept a sharp eye for any danger on the road. Before long the bright banners of the Emporium came into view.

He loved the bright colors, sounds and fascinating smells of the food stalls in the Greenbrier Emporium. Whenever he visited the Emporium, it always felt as if he were at the great festival that was held in the village center each year. He lost himself in the sea of activity and it helped salve his loneliness. The fat round body of Golika the fluff merchant always made him laugh. The fluff merchants sold everything from thistle down to dandelion fluff. On this day Golinka looked particularly ridiculous with his tall pointed cap and too tight waistcoat and pants. Golinka liked to tell jokes, and the laughter and good cheer made Piffels feel warm inside. After he hoisted the bag of thistle down over his shoulder, Piffels headed off in the direction of the seed merchants. Racks after racks of colorful seeds were arranged in rows on either side of a stone walkway. Each seed merchant specialized in a particular seed variety, and they were all competing with each other to attract customers. Passing the marigold, sunflower and onion seeds, he found Vera, the pumpkin seed merchant. Vera was an older lady elf looking particularly lovely with colorful ribbons and sparkly spangles in her graying hair, as was the custom for lady elves. She was an old friend and always allowed Piffels to hand pick the very best seeds. As Piffels was her only customer, he conducted his business quickly and wished his friend Vera a fine day. Now carrying a bag of thistle down and a package of pumpkin seeds, Piffels headed off to the fairy quarter, located at the rear of the Emporium. The fairy quarter was an open-air affair to allow the fairies a flight path. This area was a sea of activity and color, with fairies flying to and fro carrying goods from their woodland homes to sell at market. The sunlight reflecting off their gossamer iridescent wings created flashing rainbows of color. The fairies were purveyors of the finest spices, beautiful rare gems and elegant goods of all kinds. Because they lived closer to the outside world, they had access to much that was not available within the elfin lands. Piffels quickly found the spice he was looking for, but tarried a bit taking in the color and music of the fairies.

Carrying the pouch of spice and with the bag of thistle down and pumpkin seeds over his shoulder, he headed back to his home. Rather than take the main road, he decided to take the longer way home, the little path through the forest of tall flowers, the rock pile, and the marigold patch to avoid contact with anyone who might want to cause him harm. It was a rougher road to travel and it would take longer to get home, but on more than one occasion while traveling the main road he had been robbed of his purchases, and he had no desire to repeat that again. As in any society, the elf world did have its bad elements. The sun was setting over the great stonewalls by the time he delivered his packages to Esmenia.

"It's about time you got here, ya little ragmuffin," said Esmenia, grabbing the packages. "Supper in half an hour – go get cleaned up, ya look a mess – and don't leave it messy up there!"

Piffels trudged up the stairs to his little room. He carefully closed the door and lit the small lamp on the table. Nestled in a small box under his bed was a large sheet of paper carefully folded into a small rectangle. As he carefully unfolded the paper, he saw that it was much larger than the surface of the table so he rolled up the excess length. He placed two stones on the corners of the paper to hold it in place. Reaching up on a shelf, he brought down a large bottle of ink and a special brush that he had made himself just for this purpose. Dipping the brush into the ink, he began to craft large letters on the paper. Piffels had studied not only the elfin language but that of the fairies, the gnomes, and of humankind as well. Master Evergreen thought it was important that his education be as broad as possible. It was difficult to draw the letters of the humankind language large enough on the paper. He stepped back and looked at his work. Carefully printed on the paper were the words "HELLO MY NAME IS PIFFELS". Again he bent over his work and carefully printed the rest of his message, moving the paper up a bit for each line. Piffels did not see the door to his room open a bit and then quietly close again.

"Piffels, supper – come on down now!" shouted Esmenia up the stairs.

"Be right down," called Piffels, and he carefully folded the large sheet of paper and carefully packed the rectangular parcel into his knapsack. He placed the knapsack under his bed and went downstairs for supper.

ooooo

It had been a long, fun summer day and Esmeralda was enjoying watching the sunset with Granny while sitting on the big porch-swinging chair. She noticed that her grandmother seemed a little preoccupied this evening.

"Granny, is everything all right?" asked Esmeralda with a note of concern in her voice.

"Oh…. Yes my dear, it's just been a long day," said her grandmother Beverly with a note of weariness in her voice. "I think it's almost time for supper. Let's go inside now." Esmeralda helped her grandmother up from the chair just as the sun set below the horizon.

"Perfect timing you two, I was just going to call you both for supper," said Jane as they all sat down for the evening meal. It was one of Esmeralda's favorites - fried chicken with smashed potatoes and gravy with cooked carrots and peas from the garden. After supper, Esmeralda went upstairs to her little room.

She opened the window, looked out at the clear starfilled sky, and dreamed awhile of far away places. Isolated as she was out in the country, she missed having playmates to play with on a regular basis. As she looked up, a meteor flashed across the sky.

"I wish, I wish, I wish upon that falling star that someday I will have someone I can call a friend and share adventures with. I wish upon that star," said Esmeralda wistfully.

"Esmeralda, it is time for bed. I'll be right up to tuck you in," said her mother from the bottom of the stairs.

After Esmeralda had put on her nightgown and climbed into bed, her mother came into the room and closed the window a little, leaving it open just enough so the cool night breeze blew into the room. She pulled the coverlet up to her daughter's chin and kissed her on the forehead.

"Sleep tight and pleasant dreams. See you in the morning," said Jane as she closed the bedroom door and walked back down the stairs.

ooooo

As Piffels sat in his darkened room many thoughts troubled him, but the thought uppermost in his mind was the adventure on which he was about to embark. The risks were many, and then there was the elfin law that forbade any elf from going outside the great stonewalls. Outside the walls there was no protection from Fairy Glamour, that magical shield that made the elves all but invisible to the outside world. The only elves that regularly traveled to the outside world were the warrior elves. These were specially selected and trained elves and were a breed apart from the rest of elfin society. Many were the stories of foolish elves that fancied themselves to be warriors and who traveled into the outside world on their own, only to fall victim to ferocious crawling and winged beasts and were never heard from again. Piffels shivered at the thought of certain death outside the great stonewall and it was difficult for him to swallow the feeling of fear swelling in his middle. Still, his mind was made up. "Tonight is the night…I'm going," he said to himself while drawing up as much courage as he could. He pulled on his little jacket and the warm cap that Esmenia had made for him. After he threaded his belt through the top of the scabbard, he slid his elfin sword into place. Somehow he felt a little safer and braver by wearing it, not that he particularly thought of himself as a warrior elf. He pulled his knapsack over his shoulders and opened the door to his room. The house was dark and quiet as he crept silently down the stairs. As he opened the front door, Piffels did not see the concerned eyes watching him from the shadows.

It was a very quiet and cool night outside. He made his way down the main road toward the great stonewall. When he arrived at the wall, he looked for the special stone he had found earlier. As he removed the stone he could see a small opening leading to the outside world. He removed his knapsack and sword and pushed them into the opening in front of him. Squeezing into the small opening, he wiggled and squirmed his way through it. He could feel his heart beat faster as he tumbled from the opening onto the ground. Quickly he stood up, pulled his knapsack over his shoulders, and slid the sword back into its scabbard.

He found himself facing a sea of grass with blades that looked like giant green swords pointing toward the sky. He was careful to walk between the blades, as the edges were serrated and sharp. Way off in the distance was his objective, the second floor window of the humankind house. Tonight it looked like a welcoming yellow square hanging in the dark night sky. He knew from all his observations that soon that yellow light would go out, leaving him in the strange dark outside world. Strange sounds and smells filled the night air, and he could feel fear welling up inside him. Piffels began making his way through the sea of grass, the blades almost as tall as he was, and he could just barely see over the tops of them. It took him almost half the night to reach the back wall of the humankind house. Large ropy vines grew up the side of the house right past the second story bedroom window that was his objective.

"Well that was easy - I didn't see any beasts at all," Piffels said aloud in an attempt to try and push aside the fear that almost overwhelmed him. Little did Piffels know that he had spoken too soon.

As Piffels grabbed the ropy vines and began climbing up the wall of the humankind house, he heard a sound that made his little body break out in a cold sweat.

"Meeeowrrr, Meeeowwrr."

As Piffels looked over his shoulder, he saw a sight that sent a chill up his spine and made his blood run cold - a set of enormous green eyes, pointed furry ears, and teeth that looked like they could cut him in two. For a moment he hung on the vines, frozen with fear, and then began to climb as fast as his little body would carry him.

"Meeeowwrr," was the sound that came from the beast. From the corner of his eye he saw a furry blur as sharp claws ripped through his pants. Piffels climbed faster than he thought was possible. His little heart was beating so fast he thought it would burst from his chest.

After climbing for what seemed like forever, he saw the windowsill. His little arms ached and he was soaking wet with sweat. He paused to catch his breath, and then made his way through the small opening at the bottom the window. He opened his knapsack and removed a small coil of rope. After attaching one end to a small metal ring just inside the window, he lowered himself to the floor of a huge room. He walked to the leg of a large table. It was a difficult climb, but he made it to the top of the table. From that vantage point he could see the humankind child that he had observed from a distance all these years.

"Perhaps we can be friends," he said to himself as he opened his knapsack and removed the special note he had made. Carefully he unfolded it and laid it out on the table. He took one last look at what he hoped to be a friend, and climbed back down to the floor. He then climbed back up the rope to the opening at the bottom of the window. Coiling the rope up, he put it back into his knapsack. Pulling the knapsack over his shoulders, he stepped out onto the windowsill and began climbing down the ropy vines. What Piffels saw then caused his skin to prickle and fear to rise inside him, creating a taste in his mouth like bitter bile. There were three of the furry beasts waiting for him on the ground below. Something changed inside Piffels as he clung to the vines. He felt a new courage stir and rise up inside of him.

"Hey you creatures down there, I am Piffels. I am a warrior elf - prepare to meet your doom," he shouted down at the furry beasts. "Meeeowwwwrr," was the only reply.

As he reached the ground, the three furry beasts began to creep closer. Piffels drew his little elfin sword, and without another thought, charged the closest beast, sinking his sword deep into a large furry paw. "Yeeoowwwr," screamed the beast as it rolled over on its back, licking its paw. Piffels looked over his shoulder and could see the other two beasts initially shrink back and then give chase, as Piffels ran into the sea of grass. He could hear the sound of furry paws hitting the ground and the sound of large furry bodies crashing through the grass, and then the sound faded away as he continued to run toward the great stonewall way off in the distance. Piffels found himself running without thinking, oblivious to the sharp edges of the blades of grass cutting into his skin. He was just running and running, with thoughts of happy times and the calm safety of the elfin world filling his mind.

As he drew near the great stonewall he heard a new sound like someone beating the air. He looked up and saw a large winged beast with horrible sharp claws descending toward him from the sky. He weaved and darted under a large stone just as the claws were about to clamp about his little body. He was breathing so hard he felt dizzy and sick to his stomach. He looked out from under the stone and he could see the winged beast flying away into the night sky. The image of the great stonewall began to swim before his eyes and he wondered if he would ever make it safely home. It seemed that every sound and every movement spelled danger. He closed his eyes and forced himself to relax. He waited there, crouched under the stone for a little while, trying desperately to calm down and catch his breath. When he thought it safe, he made his way to the small opening in the wall and made his way back into the elfin world. Once back in his own world, he noticed that he was a mess. Soaking wet with sweat, covered with many small bloody cuts, dirty from head to foot, and his pants were in shreds. He gathered himself together and made his way down the road toward his home just as the first hints of the coming dawn lit up the night sky. After he was safely back in his little room, he immediately collapsed fully clothed onto his bed and fell fast asleep.

Later that day, as Piffels made his way down the stairs to get something to eat, Master Evergreen met him at the bottom of the stairs and asked, "Did you sleep okay last night, Piffels?"

"Yeah, I slept okay," said Piffles while stifling a yawn and nursing his sore body.

"Hmm, you must have had one hell of a dream last night, judging by the state of your clothing," said Master Evergreen with a wink.

ooooo

Esmeralda yawned, stretched and rolled out of bed, and then saw a strange small square of paper on her night table. Curious, she picked up the little piece of paper and saw the tiny words that read:

HELLO MY NAME IS PIFFELS
I AM AN ELF
I WOULD LIKE TO BE YOUR FRIEND
LOOK FOR ANOTHER MESSAGE
AT THE GARDEN STONEWALL

Esmeralda could feel an electric excitement fill her body as she ran into her grandmother's bedroom.

"Granny, Granny, look what I found in my room," said Esmeralda, waving the little note in the air.

"What is it, child?" asked Grandmother Beverly as she

took the little note from Esmeralda. As she read the note she felt shivers up her spine. She sat up in her bed and said, "Oh my God, Oh my God, Esmeralda, we need to talk. Come with me."

Chapter Two

I Want to Be Your Friend

Contact between humankind and an elf was exceedingly rare. Lost in the mists of time, there had occurred a terrible tragedy that forever separated elf and humankind. Over the centuries, elves and their kindred spirits, the fairies, had become the stuff of legends and stories told to children. Likewise, in the realm of the elves, knowledge of humankind also faded into legend and story. There were those few special elves and humankind who put aside the tragedies of the past and managed to live together in love and harmony. But these were rare and very few in number.

Holding the little note in her trembling hand, Beverly realized that she was witnessing a historical event that, if not handled properly, could result in much hurt and heart-ache, but if handled well, had the potential to heal a centu-ries-old rift between two ancient peoples. Then there was the question of her daughter, Jane, for whom elves, fairies and the like were akin to the devil. But how to handle all this properly, that was the question that troubled her mind as her grandchild sat by her side, seeking answers that she did not yet have. She put her arm around her grandchild and held her close.

"Esmeralda, remember when I told you all about the Elves and Fairies that live in our back garden? Well, it seems that an elf named Piffels wants to be your friend."

"Is Piffels a real elf?" asked Esmeralda.

"I think so. It looks like someone about the size of an elf went through a whole lot of trouble to leave you this little note. It is not very often that elves make contact with us. Fortune has smiled on you, child. I do not why the elves have chosen this time to come among us, nor do I know why they chose you."

"I feel a little frightened, Granny," said Esmeralda, hold-ing her grandmother very close.

"It's alright; there is really nothing to be afraid of. I will go with you to the garden and together we will see about Piffels. We should not tell your mother about all this right now. It will be our special secret, okay?"

"Okay Granny, our special secret," said Esmeralda, nod-ding her head and putting her finger to her lips.

Beverly put the little note in her pocket and thought to herself, "I must talk with Elron immediately about all this."

Later that morning, making sure that no one noticed she had left the house, Beverly went to the appointed spot next to the stone wall surrounding the back garden. She placed her hands on the glass garden gazing ball and recited the ancient magical chant.

"Wickedy Wackady Woo
Ding Dong Felron
Make me just as small
As Elron"

She never could get used to that electrical prickly feeling no matter how many times she had made this journey.

Relaxing, as he was in his study, Elron Evergreen was startled to see his humankind friend Beverly appear next him in a shower of sparkles and tinkling sounds. "Beverly! I am surprised to see you. You did not send advanced word that you would be coming," he said. He arose from his chair and carefully locked the door to the study.

"What brings you here in such a rush, my friend?" he said as he wrapped a blanket around the elderly woman.

"Elron, contact has been made!" said Beverly breathlessly, with a troubled look on her face.

"Contact? With whom?"

"My granddaughter, Esmeralda."

"When did this contact take place?" Elron Evergreen said with genuine concern in his voice.

"Last night. Esmeralda found this note on her dressing table this morning," Beverly said, as she handed Elron Evergreen the heavy folded paper. He carefully unfolded the large note, laid it out on the floor, and read the hand-lettered message.

HELLO MY NAME IS PIFFELS
I AM AN ELF
I WOULD LIKE TO BE YOUR FRIEND

LOOK FOR ANOTHER MESSAGE
AT THE GARDEN STONEWALL

"Piffels! Damn! So that is where that little dingus went last night!" Elron Evergreen said with anger in his voice. "I will get to the bottom of this!" he said. He unlocked the door to the study and shouted down the stairs to Esmenia to send Piffels up to the study immediately.

Piffels walked up the stairs to the Master's study. 'What could Master Evergreen want at this hour?' he thought to himself. As Piffels entered the study, he felt his mouth go dry and he could feel the sweat beading up on his body. Nausea washed over him like a wave of icy water. There standing next to Master Evergreen was an old humankind woman who was now elf-size. Not just any humankind woman, but the grandmother that he observed so many times from the human house. 'But how can this be?' he thought to himself. 'Surely no one knows of my visit last night.' Then he saw his hand-lettered note laid-out on the floor and he felt genuinely ill!

"Well, how do you explain this?" asked Master Evergreen, with his hands on his hips and a stern look on his face.

"But Master, I ... I was looking for a friend, I was curious about the humankind world," said Piffels, backing up a bit and looking furtively at the humankind woman.

"Well, being curious is one thing, but acting on that curiosity is quite another. Did you think about the consequences of this contact with the human world?" asked Elron, looking sterner than before.

"Consequences? I ... I don't understand. What do you mean - consequences?" asked Piffels, backing up a little more.

Master Evergreen's face took on a more fatherly look as he said, "Piffels, come sit down. We need to talk. There is much that you do not know or understand."

All three, Master Evergreen, Piffels, and the elderly humankind woman, sat down on chairs in the dimly lit study. No one noticed the pair of elfin eyes peering through the partially opened studio door; nor did they notice the studio door silently closing.

Master Evergreen filled his pipe with herbal blend, set it alight, and puffed on it, filling the air with a gray haze. He sat back in his chair and looked at Piffels much as a schoolmaster to a pupil. He motioned to the humankind woman and said, "Let me introduce you to my friend Beverly. She is a sort of humankind ambassador to our elfin world. We have been friends for a very long time."

"I am happy to meet you, Piffels. I have known Elron Evergreen for most of my life. We first met when I was but a child, and I count him as a good and trusted friend," said Beverly, giving Elron a warm smile.

"Let me tell you a story of long, long ago, when humankind and elf kind walked freely among each other," said Master Evergreen as he puffed on his pipe. A wreath of pale smoke hung over his head like a pale blue-gray halo. "Those were happy times with much knowledge and trade exchanged between worlds. Then greed took over both humankind and elf as both began to covet the possessions of the other. Some of the humankind greatly desired the elfin lands and some elves greatly desired the gold and precious things in the humankind world. Some in the humankind world decimated entire elf villages in an insane desire for the fertile lands of the elves. The elves had little defense against the humankind onslaught. The fairies came to the aid of the elves and bestowed upon us the gift of fairy glamour, the ability to make ourselves invisible to humankind and other creatures of this world. One constraint is that the fairy glamour only works if high rock walls enclose the lands. Any elf stepping outside of the protected area becomes visible, and most likely prey to other creatures of the humankind world."

'So that explains the high rock walls around our village of Greenbrier,' Piffels thought to himself, 'And that also explains the furry and winged beasts I encountered.' He felt a chill remembering just how close he had come to death.

Beverly leaned forward, looking at Piffels, and said, "Over time, contact between the worlds was lost, and to humankind, elves became a thing of myth and legend. At the same time, to the elves, humans became fearful evil creatures that also became a thing of myth and legend. Throughout the land of the elves, contact with humankind was forbidden and a tradition of non contact was established."

Beverly looked over at Master Evergreen and he said, "There were always a few of humankind and of the elfin world who sought contact, to try and heal the rift between the worlds."

Beverly looked at Piffels with a kindness in her eyes and said, "Your making contact with my world is not inherently a bad thing, but it could, if not handled properly, upset the delicate balance between the worlds and could cause harm to many."

Silence filled the studio like a heavy fog, and finally Piffels sat up in his chair and, looking straight at both Beverly and Master Evergreen, said in a firm, confident voice, "What is it that I need to do? I did not know of these things you speak of. I did not know."

Master Evergreen looked at his young student and thought to himself, "Hmmm, there is something different about Piffels. Something strong awakened inside him during his visit to the outside world."

Chapter Three

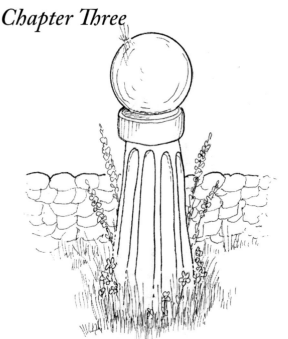

Hello My Name Is Esmeralda

Esmeralda always liked the fiery sunsets of midsummer. As she sat next to her grandmother and gazed at the fiery orange ball dipping below the horizon, she imagined that the fireflies flashing in the gathering twilight were the fairies that Granny had told her so much about. She felt the chill of the evening, pulled her shawl over her shoulders, and snuggled up against her grandmother.

"Esmeralda, let me tell you about the elves," said Grandmother Beverly as she sat Esmeralda on her lap. She took a long sip of her tea and then continued, "A long, long time ago humankind, people that looked just like us, lived side by side with the elves. Each one helping each other enjoy rich full lives."

"You mean elves were real back then?" said Esmeralda looking up at her grandmother.

"Well yes, in fact - they are very real and with us today."

"Today, here – now?"

"Yes, here now," said Grandmother Beverly with a dreamy faraway look in her eyes.

"But why can't we see them?"

"Because of something terrible that happened so long ago. The elves decided to make themselves invisible to most of humankind and have lived apart from us for a very long time. But now a young elf has decided to break with that long tradition. A little elf named ... Piffels."

"The Piffels from my little note?" said Esmeralda excitedly.

"Yes indeed, the very same Piffels."

"What do elves look like? Are they just like us?"

Grandmother Beverly reached into her large knit purse and pulled out a large book. "Well – first of all, elves are very small, usually no larger that your hand," said Grandmother Beverly as she opened the book. "Here, I have some pictures of elves."

Displayed on the pages of the book were several color drawings of elves. Grandmother Beverly placed the open book on Esmeralda's lap.

"Oh look! They look kind of brown and they all have pointy ears!" exclaimed Esmeralda as she excitedly turned the pages, looking at more color drawings of elves. "Why do some have bows and sparkly things in their hair?"

"Those are girl elves," said Grandmother Beverly chuckling. "All the girl elves make themselves pretty by dressing up their hair."

"Oh how awesome, I would like to dress up my hair too!" said Esmeralda emphatically.

"And so you shall, my child … and so you shall. But first, let me tell you some other things you need to know about elves."

ooooo

Piffels loved the coming of night – that special twilight time when it was neither quite day nor night, but a magical in-between time when fantasy and wonder seemed to permeate the air. He especially liked to spend this time sitting in the big chairs on the front porch of his home with Master Evergreen. Many were the stories of times long ago that Master Evergreen would tell amidst the aroma of the herbal blend that he loved to smoke in his pipe. Piffels snuggled up in the soft warmth of the big chair and pulled a small blanket around his shoulders against the chill of the night air.

"Piffels – let me tell you about humankind. By the way, I have seen all those notebooks you have carefully stored in the secret place in the observatory cupboards. Nice observations … and excellent drawings I might add – but there is much that your observations do not tell you," said Master Evergreen as he puffed on his pipe. He reached into a large box and pulled out a large book and gave it to Piffels. As he opened the book, Piffels saw color drawings of all sorts of humankind.

"Hmmm, interesting - some have darker skin than the human kind that I have observed in the big house," said Piffels as he turned the pages while drinking in the images.

"Yes, very observant, Piffels. There is much more variety in the humankind world than in our own elfin world. Some are tall, short, fat, skinny and all sorts of shades of color – but they are all humankind."

"I have not seen this book before," said Piffels caressing the binding of the book.

"This is the book of Round Ears … one of the forbidden books. All other copies of this book were destroyed when elves and human kind went separate ways … you must never tell anyone that you have seen this book!" said Master Evergreen, looking directly at Piffels with a serious, stern look. "There are many who would stop at nothing to keep humankind and elf separate."

"But why? That does not make any sense to me when there was a time when elf and humankind walked together as brothers," said Piffels with a pained look.

"Piffels … It is sad, but sometimes old fears and hatreds live very long lives," said Master Evergreen with a look of sadness on his face. "The humankind – elf contact you are about to make would be violently opposed by many in both the elfin and humankind worlds – we must be very, very careful."

"I understand, and I will be very careful." Piffels closed the book and looked up at Master Evergreen. "I have a question. How is it that humankind can travel between our two worlds? I saw the lady Beverly in the library. How did she become small like us? And why was she not wearing any clothing?"

"Ah yes … Piffels ever the curious," said Master Evergreen with a chuckle. "First, let me say that over the long time that humankind and elf have been separate, much wisdom and knowledge has been lost. There was a time, long ago, that the elves were considered a very advanced culture. But that was a long time in the past."

Master Evergreen re-lit his pipe, sat back in his chair and puffed for a minute before he continued. "Centuries ago, elves of wisdom discovered a way to bend reality to allow the transfer of matter from one state of reality to another – from the world of humankind to our world, for example. Unfortunately, the intimate details of how and why it works have been lost to the mists of time, and there are only a few of us left who know how to use it. You discovered, in your adventure outside the stonewalls, that we can move from one world to the other in our own size rather easily. It is becoming large like humankind or small like the elves that is difficult."

"Can you teach me how to use this transfer of reality?" asked Piffels, his face all lit up with interest.

"In time, when you are ready, I will teach you what you need to know so that when I am gone the knowledge will live on. - Now as to the second part of your question, the transfer only works with living things, such as humans, elves, animals and so on. Clothing, not being a living thing, stays behind in the transfer."

"Hmmm … I see. So because the visit of Lady Beverly was unplanned, there was no elf clothing for her to wear after her transfer. But how would you know that she wanted to transfer? How are messages sent back and forth between the worlds?"

"Questions, questions! Messages between the worlds are a difficult thing. Written messages, much as you used in your little adventure, are the usual way to communicate at first. However, once contact between humankind and elf is made, a mental link is established that allows messages of a sort to be exchanged between the worlds," said Master Evergreen as he looked directly at Piffels. "You too will learn about this in time – it is a gift that we elves possess."

"I have one other question. Who is the Master?" asked Piffels leaning forward in his chair.

Master Evergreen puffed on his pipe, sat back in his chair and said, "The Master, as he wishes to be called, is also known by his elfin name of Frankenflick. He was once known as Master Trueblood, a highly respected Daemon. He is the last of the human/elf half-breeds, and as such he was an ambassador, a link between the humankind world and the world of the elves. His father was humankind and his mother was an elf. This was at a time when elves and humankind walked together as brothers. However, there were some in the humankind world who saw this mixed race family as a threat to their way of life and subjected Frankenflick and his family to the most awful discrimination and mistreatment. His mother was killed by a humankind mob and his father was subjected to exile where he died a broken man. Deeply hurt and fearing for his life, Frankenflick escaped to the world of the elves and forswore any allegiance to the humankind world. The Master has harbored a deep-seated hatred of all things humankind. This hatred has poisoned his soul to the point where even the elves have grown to look upon him and his followers with deep distrust. Although he is still considered a member of the Council of Elder Elves, he is held apart from most of elfin society."

"Squashnosh! Looks like I have much to learn. I did not realize how complicated all this would be," said Piffels, rubbing his head with his hands.

'You really have no idea just how much you will learn – no idea at all,' thought Master Evergreen to himself.

"Piffels, come with me, as we have many preparations to make." Master Evergreen stood up and motioned for Piffels to follow him.

ooooo

It was very quiet in the back garden of the Hathaway house on this late summer morning. The sun was just coming up over the horizon and the grass was still wet with dew. Birds were just beginning to sing and the insects were beginning to stir in the cool morning air. It was as if the earth was slowly waking up from the nighttime slumber.

Nestled in a small, secluded circle of shrubs and trees on the backside of the garden there stood a marble pedestal, and a large glass gazing ball in the very center of the small circle.

"Esmeralda – come child, it is almost time," said Grandmother Beverly as she motioned for Esmeralda to stand by her side in the center of the circle. "Do you remember what we talked about?"

"Uh huh. Yes Granny, I remember."

Esmeralda felt a feeling of excitement rise up inside her as she placed her hands on the gazing ball. "Okay Granny, I am ready," she said with excitement in her voice.

Although Beverly had made this trip more times than she could remember, taking her granddaughter with her made this trip different indeed. "Alright now, let's say the chant together."

> "Whoosh, whoosh tingles
> Sparkle in the Jingle
> Poof, Poof Diffles
> Make me just as small as Piffels"

The sound of tinkling bells, the strong smell of flowers, and a tingling tickling feeling washed over them. Esmeralda giggled and squeaked with glee at the wonder of it all. The garden began to slowly disappear, to be replaced by a gray misty fog. The mist quickly began to disappear and they found themselves in another garden surrounded by tall tree trunks, shrubs that looked like huge green swords sticking out in all directions, and several large and tall stones. A large two-story cottage slowly appeared out of the receding mist. As Esmeralda looked up she realized that these were not tree trunks, but the stems of tall flowers. The interlocking leaves and petals of the flowers were acting like huge colorful parasols shielding them from the morning sun.

"Esmeralda – quickly put on this robe," said Grandmother Beverly as she handed her granddaughter a brown robe made from woven tree bark fiber. Esmeralda, realizing that she had no clothes on, quickly grabbed the robe, put it on and pulled it close around her. The robe felt warm and very silky soft. Just then a tall, gray-haired elf with pointy ears and a snowy white full beard stepped out from behind one the large stones. He was dressed in a green jacket, brown shirt, and pants.

Esmeralda tugged on her grandmother's sleeve and said in a loud whisper, "Granny, there's an elf here!"

"Greetings, I am Elron Evergreen. So this must be Esmeralda … My word, Beverly, she does have your eyes," said Master Evergreen. Just then a small elf peeked around from behind Master Evergreen's legs.

"Oh Piffels, do come on out. I don't think she is going to bite!" said Master Evergreen with a chuckle. The little elf slowly and tentatively walked out in front of Master Evergreen and then stopped, looked down at the ground, and shuffled his feet.

'Oh snickelswish! It is one thing to observe humankind, but it is quite another to have them here … now … right in front of me! Why does this humankind woman child make me feel so funny inside?' thought Piffels to himself.

"Hello … my name is Esmeralda. Are you Piffels?" Esmeralda said while holding on to her grandmother.

"Hi … I … I am glad to meet you … my … my name is P - P… Piffels. I … I would like to be your friend," Piffels said, looking at Esmeralda with a hopeful look on his face, and wondering to himself why it was that he found it so difficult to talk all of a sudden.

Esmeralda looked up at her grandmother, who winked back at her, and then Esmeralda said, "Yes, I would love to be your friend." She reached out and gave Piffels a big hug. Master Evergreen was sure that was the first time he ever saw Piffels blush!

"Well then, that's all settled, let us all go up into the house. Some proper elf clothes and I think some morning food is in order," said Master Evergreen, motioning everyone up the small hill to the back of the cottage. The two-story cottage was covered with a white stucco-like coating with thin transparent sheets of mica in the windows. The roof was made of interlocking layers of a brown grass thatch. The edges of the thatch were closely trimmed, giving the edge of the roof a neat and trim appearance. A heavy wooden door led into the rear of the cottage.

Once inside, Master Evergreen gave Esmeralda a green shirt, green pants, and a pretty tan jacket with flowers painted on it. On her feet were fitted mouse leather shoes that felt a lot like soft, warm slippers. He explained that both male and female elves wear pretty much the same clothes, except that the female elves decorate their clothing with designs or flowers. Then he placed a wig on Esmeralda's head that had the hair all teased out elf fashion in a poofy bunch. Fastened to the hair were pretty, colorful bows and sparkling spangles that caught the light and glittered. As he fitted the wig so that it covered her ears, he explained that female elves always took pride in the decorations that they tied in their hair. Girl elves that had not made the transition to womanhood wore green ribbons in their hair, while female elves that were of age wore red ribbons in their hair, red being the symbol of elfin womanhood.

Next, her grandmother carefully applied some coloring to her skin to darken it slightly so she looked more like an elf. Esmeralda looked at herself in the mirror and saw looking back at her a little girl elf with sparkling spangles and green ribbons in her hair. Grandmother Beverly stood next to her, looking very much like an elf matron with red ribbons in her gray, poofy wig.

"Granny, do I look like an elf?"

"Indeed you do child, indeed you do."

"Proper elves you both are indeed. Now we need to give you an elf name," said Master Evergreen as he placed his hand on Esmeralda's shoulder.

"Twinkles is your name while you are with us. Twinkles Pink Blossom is your new formal name, or just Twinkles amongst friends."

"Twinkles, I love it!" said Piffels as he stood next to his new friend.

"What is my Grandmother's elfin name?" said Esmeralda.

"Myra, Myra Silver Stone is my elf name," said Grandmother Beverly, smiling and putting her arm around her granddaughter.

"Happy to meet you, Myra Silver Stone," said Piffels, giving a respectful little bow. "Twinkles and Myra it is then, my new elfin friends."

"Now we have the matter of language. Both Piffels and I speak your humankind language. However, most elves only speak the ancient elf tongue. If you are to move easily among us and learn our ways, you must be able to understand and speak as we do. Are you ready and willing to truly become an elf for as long as you are with us?" asked Master Evergreen, looking deeply into Esmeralda's eyes.

"Yes … yes, I am ready," said Esmeralda with a note of anticipation in her voice. She looked up at her Grandmother who smiled, nodded yes, and winked back at her.

"Very well then, hold out your hands and close your eyes. When you next open them, an elf you will be for as long as you are in the land of the elves."

Master Evergreen grasped Esmeralda's hands, closed his eyes, and recited an ancient elfin chant; "Myloar Dundus Fuorloureen Gamaloureen Thoral Thoral … An elf you are in speech, thought and all for as long as you are in this world … Gamaloureen Thoral Thoral!"

Twinkles felt a tingling sensation run up through her arms and into her head. Thousands of images instantly flashed through her mind and then – all was quiet.

"What is your name?" asked Master Evergreen in the ancient elfin tongue.

"My name is Twinkles Pink Blossom of village Dundeen," said Twinkles confidently.

"Good, good," said Master Evergreen.

Twinkles could not understand what all the fuss was about her name; her name had always been Twinkles.

"Now I must tell you about Esmenia, our housekeeper," said Master Evergreen, looking very serious. "Esmenia is a good sort, but she does not take well to strangers in her house."

"It is probably best that you let me do most of the talking," said Piffels, now looking very brave and strangely protective.

"Okay then, if you are ready for the adventure to begin, let us share a morning meal," said Master Evergreen, while motioning them all to follow him up the stairs

A small upstairs room served as both kitchen and dining room. A round wooden table sat on one end of the room, and a large metal wood-fired stove dominated the other end. As the elves have no knowledge of electricity, home appliances, like refrigerators, toasters and the like do not exist in the elfin world. Instead, braided sheaves of grasses and dried plants hung from the ceiling. The walls on either side of the kitchen stove were taken up with a floor-to-ceiling pantry. Shelves in the pantry held crockery pots filled with all manner of herbs and spices. Pullout pantry bins were filled with dried mushrooms, flower petals, and seeds of every description. In the center wall of the kitchen was a large pot filled with water fed from a roof-mounted cistern. A large metal pot of spicy sunflower seed porridge was on the stove with its contents quietly bubbling. Esmenia, the housekeeper, dressed in a brown house gown and apron, was standing next to the stove stirring the porridge with a large wooden spoon. The savory aroma of the spicy porridge filled the room.

"Esmenia, we have guests for the morning meal," said Master Evergreen as everyone filed into the little dining room.

"Well I hope I have made enough for everyone!" said Esmenia with a note of irritation in her voice. "I wish you would have let me know. I could have tidied up a bit more."

"Well, our guests arrived at the last minute. I apologize for the short notice. Piffels, set the table," said Master Evergreen with a smile, as he motioned for everyone to be seated.

Piffels set out wooden bowls, wooden spoons, and big ceramic mugs for everyone. Esmenia brought the pot of steaming porridge and set it on the table. She placed a large pitcher of water and a platter loaded with a warm loaf of bread on the table.

"I just baked the loaf of pumpkin seed bread this morning," said Esmenia as she sat down at the table.

"You are a dear heart, thank you Esmenia. Let me introduce you to our guests. This is Twinkles Pink Blossom and her grandmother Myra Silver Stone visiting us from village Dundeen. Myra is the Daemon of Dundeen." Master Evergreen paused, and with a warm smile said, "Myra and Twinkles, this is Esmenia Rangle Root of Greenbrier, my housekeeper,"

"I am so happy to meet you, Esmenia. You have a lovely, warm home. Elron is very fortunate to have you," said Myra.

"Dundeen eh! That is a long way from here. What brings you to Greenbrier?" said Esmenia, her eyes narrowly looking at the two visitors.

"We are on our way to the village of Rosethorn to visit some old friends," said Myra as she sampled the porridge. "My goodness Esmenia, I must compliment you on a very delicious morning meal.

"Ummff, and what of you, Twinkles?" said Esmenia, fixing her narrowing gaze on Twinkles.

"She is Myra's granddaughter," said Piffels, quickly jumping in.

"Ummff, so Twinkles cannot speak for herself?" said Esmenia while glaring at Piffels.

'There is something just not quite right about these two,' Esmenia thought to herself. She had heard the persistent rumors of round ears invading the elfin lands, and wondered if Evergreen was somehow involved in this, and then there was that strange woman in Evergreen's study.

"I am traveling with my grandmother to learn about some of the other villages. My grandmother feels it would be a good education for me," said Twinkles as she busied herself breaking a crust of bread and eating the porridge.

'Hmmm, a good answer. This human child thinks well on her feet,' thought Master Evergreen to himself.

"Ummmff, well then welcome, and I hope your trip is without difficulty," said Esmenia, turning her attention to her bowl of porridge, all the while looking at these two visitors out of the corner of her eye.

"Well then, eat up everyone, we have a busy day ahead," said Master Evergreen.

The meal was finished while Myra Silver Stone and Elron Evergreen exchanged small talk, with Esmenia in the background continuing to stare at the visitors suspiciously.

Esmeralda was very uncomfortable. The wig was itchy and it was all she could do not to scratch under it. And then there were the nasty looks from Esmenia. This lady elf just made her feel all icky and uncomfortable. At least the porridge was very rich and spicy, and the bread was the very best she had ever tasted. She would be very happy to be out from under the gaze of Esmenia.

Piffels could sense that his new friend was uncomfortable and was doing his best to help her feel welcomed, though the icy glares from Esmenia were like a splash of cold water on his efforts. He would be glad to be outside and away from this situation. He busied himself cleaning the table and motioned for his new friend to help him.

"Okay everyone, I think we will be on our way," said Master Evergreen as he arose from the table and motioned for his guests to follow him down the stairs to the front door of the cottage.

Outside the cottage, a small carriage was waiting with two gray mice hitched to it. Their long tails were curled up and held in place with large, colorful ribbons. Everyone took a seat in the carriage as Master Evergreen urged the mice forward.

As the carriage disappeared down the dirt road, Esmenia stood outside the cottage front door, wiped her hands on her apron and thought to herself, 'There is something just not right about these visitors. I must talk to Raggles Chickweed about this.'

Chapter Four

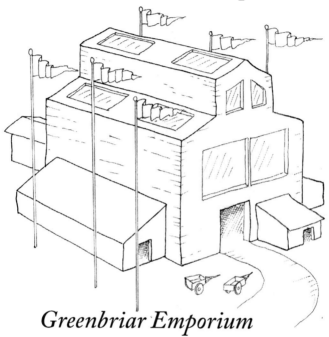

Greenbriar Emporium

The gentle rocking motion of the cart imparted by the loping gait of the two mice lulled Esmeralda into a very relaxed state. She thought back over the fantastic events of the last day. What a kind, gentle and wise man was Master Evergreen, and how cute was Piffels. She felt strangely safe and happy when she was with that little elf. The wig had become less itchy and she found herself sometime forgetting that she was wearing it. She remembered hearing her grandmother use a special word to describe a difficult woman ... what was that word? Oh yes ... Shrew! Yes, that was a good word for Esmenia!

The sounds and aromas of the Emporium reached them

even before they could see the tall poles carrying the colorful banners and the Emporium itself.

"The Greenbrier Emporium is kind of a town square, outdoor market and entertainment complex all rolled into one place," said Master Evergreen as the large barn like building came into view. "Here you will see a real cross section of elfin society, and then, there are the fairies."

"I'm going to meet some real fairies!" exclaimed Twinkles, clapping her hands with excitement.

Master Evergreen pointed to his right and said, "Just over there is the town of Greenbrier. All those cottages surrounded by the tall daisy and marigold flowers are the center of the town. Although you can't see it from here, the town square is behind that small hill and just beyond the first line of cottages."

To Twinkles, the cottages of Greenbrier town looked an awful lot like so many white and brown mushrooms scattered amongst the flowers. She tried to imagine what the town square looked like, and wondered if it looked anything like the little town close to her home in the humankind world.

Master Evergreen drove the cart to a holding pen just outside of the Emporium. Piffels unhitched the two mice from the cart and moved them into a side door in the barn like building. A worker elf led the mice into a stall where they were given water and some grain.

"Alright then, that is taken care of, let us have some fun in the Emporium," said Master Evergreen. "Piffels, you stay close to Twinkles; she is your responsibility."

"I understand. I will not let anything happen to her," said Piffels, pulling himself up and looking very much the warrior elf.

The Greenbrier Emporium was an imposing wooden building, looking very much like a huge barn. Roof mounted skylights covered with transparent sheets of mica allowed bright shafts of sunlight to illuminate the cavernous interior. Tall poles attached to the outside side of the building were adorned with colorful banners and flags representing the various merchants that did business inside the Emporium.

As the four friends walked into the large entrance portal, Twinkles was almost overcome with the sheer spectacle before her eyes. There were more elves than she could ever have imagined. A virtual flood of variations in height, weight, and girth as well as a wild cacophony of sound, color and aromas was displayed before her. Inside, the Emporium was divided into roughly equal square sections, with each section displaying a different elfin commodity. The dirt floor of the Emporium was covered with a thick layer of straw that effectively kept down the dust. Merchants in each of the commodity sections wore different color clothing. There were the fish merchants selling all sorts of aquatic creatures caught in the stream that flowed through the elfin lands. Everything from tadpoles, fish and aquatic plants were on display in specially prepared bins. These merchants were dressed all in red, from their jaunty red caps to the pointy red shoes on their feet. A corner of this area was set aside for freshly cooked aquatic foods. The sounds and smells of food cooking reminded Twinkles that it had been some time since the morning meal.

"Piffels, could I sample some of the food?"

"Well, what looks good to you?" asked Piffels, reaching into his pouch of exchange stones.

"Master Evergreen, Twinkles is hungry. Would you and

Lady Silverstone like some food?" asked Piffels.

"No, we are not hungry right now; you and Twinkles enjoy a quick meal. We will meet you at the Fairy quarter a bit later," said Master Evergreen. He and Myra Silverstone walked off into the Emporium. "Have fun, you two," he said over his shoulder.

"That looks yummy," said Twinkles, pointing to a fried fish and carrot root dish arranged on a section of lettuce leaf.

"I'll take two of those and two mugs of berry juice," said Piffels to the fish merchant, pointing to the fried fish and carrot root dish.

"That will be two stones," said the merchant.

Piffels gave the merchant the two exchange stones, and he and Twinkles sat down at a small table and enjoyed the food. Twinkles found it very juicy and flavorful, with a delightful crunch. The berry juice was sweet, with just enough tartness to make it interesting.

After finishing the food, they came to the fluff merchants all dressed in brown pointy hats, waistcoats and pants. Here were displayed bins overflowing with thistle down, milkweed fluff, dandelion down, and other fluffy materials of all kinds. Piffels introduced Twinkles to Golinka, the rotund fluff merchant. Twinkles could not help but giggle at how ridiculous Golinka looked with his pointy hat and too tight waistcoat and pants. His rosy chubby cheeks wore a constant smile. Golinka loved to tell jokes and soon had both Piffels and Twinkles laughing and enjoying themselves. After saying goodbye to Golinka and the fluff merchants, they continued on inside the Emporium.

Various shades of green and rounded caps identified the seed merchants. Row after row of a bewildering variety of seeds were all set out in wooden bins. Each bin was watched over by a merchant who specialized in that specific seed variety. Piffels introduced Twinkles to his friend Vera, the pumpkin seed merchant. Twinkles thought she looked a lovely older lady elf. She had red bows and spangles in her gray hair and a very pretty deep green jacket and pants. Twinkles blushed a bit when Vera told her she was a very pretty young lady elf. Vera gave them both a sample of pumpkin seed butter on jingle bread. Twinkles thought to herself that it tasted a lot like what she remembered peanut butter tasting like.

Thanking Vera, Piffels and Twinkles walked over to the metal smith area. Arrayed on tables were all sorts of pretty hair and clothing spangles and small metal implements of all kinds. These merchants were all dressed in orange with large brown mouse leather aprons. Very muscular looking elves were working at forges and pounding hot metal on anvils. The ringing of hammers on anvils provided an interesting percussion beat to the collection of sounds echoing off of the high ceiling in the Emporium.

"Ooh, that looks pretty!" exclaimed Twinkles, picking up a sparkling spangle from the table.

"That is a jacket spangle that you wear on your clothing instead of your hair," explained Piffels as he caught the attention of one of the metal smith merchants. "How much for this spangle?"

"Now that is a nice one … twelve stones is the price," said the merchant.

Piffels reached into his pouch and counted out six stones. The merchant saw the crestfallen look on Piffels face.

"Special deal today, for the pretty lady … only six stones," said the merchant with a smile.

Piffels counted out his last six stones and gave them to the merchant. Twinkles, realizing the sacrifice that Piffels had made, gave him a big hug and a kiss on the cheek.

"Thank you Piffels, thank you so much. It is very beautiful," said Twinkles with a tear in her eye.

"Ah young elves, ya gotta love em," said the metal smith merchant with a chuckle as he handed the spangle to Piffels.

He attached the spangle to Twinkles' jacket and stepped back to see how it looked on her.

"She does look pretty; an excellent choice, my young elf!" said the metal smith merchant.

Piffels and Twinkles then set off for the far side of the Emporium, to the woven goods and cloth merchants. As they approached the display of brightly colored cloth they saw that a demonstration was in progress. Two elves of the woven goods guild were demonstrating how fibers were beaten from tree bark and plant stems and then spun into yarn. Another set of elves was demonstrating how the fiber yarn was woven into cloth. There was a large crowd of elves gathered around the demonstration. As Piffels and Twinkles were making their way through the crowd for a better look, Piffels heard a voice that made his blood run cold.

"Yo, ya little glomsquach, I see you have found yourself a delicious little gumdrop. Hey you, I'm talking to you," said Raggles as he grabbed Piffels by the arm and wheeled him around.

"Who is that?" asked Twinkles with a concerned look on her face.

"Oh, nobody of importance," said Piffels. He took Twinkles' arm and turned away from Raggles to try and disappear into the crowd. Raggles grabbed him again and pushed him to the ground. The entire crowd turned to see what the fuss was about. Piffels started to get back up, his face burning with embarrassment, and he felt a real concern for the safety of Twinkles.

"I'm taking this delicious gumdrop! She is mine now! You pathetic little ..." Raggles did not see the wicked right hook coming at him from the side. Twinkles put all her weight into the punch as it connected with Raggles' jaw, making a sickening smacking sound as he sank to the ground like a limp rag doll. Raggles sat on the ground shaking his head, desperately trying to make sense out of what had just happened.

"This is one gumdrop that you will never have the pleasure of knowing, you pathetic excuse for an elf!" exclaimed Twinkles, as she looked down at Raggles with genuine fire in her eyes.

"It is about time someone put down that bully!" exclaimed several elves from the crowd. Piffels brushed himself off, grabbed Twinkles by the hand, and pulled her into the crowd.

"We have to go! Where did you learn to do that?" asked Piffels, breathing hard as he directed Twinkles through the crowd to the other side.

"I don't know! It was just something that I felt needed to be done," said Twinkles. Hand in hand, they quickly made their way to the fairy section at the back area of the Emporium.

Twinkles was excited about meeting the fairies that her Granny had told her so much about. She had an image in her mind of what a fairy looked like. It is interesting how sometimes reality and preconceptions do not match. To Twinkles, fairies were just elves with wings. As she and

Piffels rounded a corner into the fairy quarter, the idea of elves with wings was quickly put away. In reality, fairies are very slender and much taller than elves, with very fine delicate features and those wings! Fairy wings of every description; some looked like dragonfly wings, some like butterfly wings and some, well, for some there were just no words to describe them.

As Piffels and Twinkles walked into the fairy quarter, Piffels shared his knowledge of fairies. He explained, "In terms of scent, elves and fairies are very different. Elves have a decidedly earthy scent, much like the clean, spicy scent of the outdoors. Fairies, on the other hand, have a decidedly flowery scent, much like the rich scent of carnations mixed with the sweet smell of roses. Fairies are also fond of using perfumed smoke or incense to sweeten their environment." Piffels paused, and then continued, "Wherever you find fairies, you will find music. Drums and a variety of string and wind instruments are favorite music makers for the fairies."

Twinkles walked hand in hand with Piffels, taking in the magic around her.

"Mode of dress is another distinguishing feature between elves and fairies," said Piffels as he continued. "Elves are almost always dressed in pants and shirts in various colors and often, when the air is colder, the preferred dress is waistcoats or jackets. Elves almost always dress their feet in shoes carved from seeds or made from tanned mouse leather. Hats are also very popular, especially amongst male elves. Female elves most commonly have their hair teased out and bedecked with colored bows and sparkly spangles. In contrast to the elves, both male and female fairies wear their hair long and are usually seen wearing dried flower hats that are normally fitted with chinstraps to keep the hat in place when the fairy is in flight. Fairies almost always appear in one piece flowing gown-like attire in pastel colors. Male fairies are fond of the hotter colors of reds, yellows and oranges, while female fairies are fond of the cooler colors of blue, green and cyan. It is a beautiful sight to see fairies in flight, gowns fluttering in the breeze and the sunlight glinting off of the fluttering wings. Unlike the elves, fairies are almost always barefoot." Piffels finished sharing his knowledge of elves and fairies just as the fairy quarter came into full view.

"The fairies, they are so beautiful," said Twinkles, her eyes wide in amazement.

"I know - I never grow tired of watching them. I have always wished that I too could fly like they do ... so graceful and elegant," said Piffels as he grasped Twinkles hand and urged her on into the fairy quarter.

Tables were arranged just inside the Emporium building with a large open area to the rear that allowed the fairies to fly in and out. In the corners of the fairy quarter were tall tripod stands carrying charcoal braziers from which flowery perfumed smoke wafted over the area, creating a light blue sweet smelling haze. In one corner of the fairy quarter were four fairies in an ensemble with drums, two flutes and a large stringed instrument. Beautiful haunting melodies with a driving drum beat floated out over the entire area. There seemed to be a constant stream of fairies flying in, carrying bundles of goods from their homes in the forest, and an equal number of fairies flying out toward the distant forest. Large crowds of elves were clustered around the each of the tables, busily purchasing or trading elfin goods for rare spices, seeds, and mushrooms that only grow in the forest. And then there were the rare gems and stones gathered by the fairies from the humankind world. While the elves had separated themselves from the world of humankind, the fairies had always maintained contact with the larger world.

"Piffels! My goodness, it has been a long time. Come here and let me look at you. Has that old task master Evergreen been treating you well?" said a tall male fairy as he put his hands on Piffels' shoulders. He was an imposing sight, tall and slender, dressed in a pastel red robe, dried daisy hat, and iridescent gossamer dragonfly wings.

"Ebermarl, my old friend, so happy to see you again," said Piffels as he warmly grasped the male fairy's hand. "Master Evergreen has taught me much and I continue to learn."

"And who is this delightful little elf with you?"

"This is my friend, Twinkles Pink Blossom of Dundeen. She and her grandmother are visiting Greenbrier on their way to another village," said Piffels as he put his arm around Twinkles.

"Twinkles, this is my good fairy friend Ebermarl. We have known each other ever since I was but a wee bobbin."

"Ebermarl … I … I am so h…h…happy to meet you," said Twinkles, suddenly feeling both excited and flustered about actually talking to a fairy.

"Hmmm, Yes … yes indeed," Ebermarl said as he walked around Twinkles carefully, looking at her from head to foot. "Hmmm, yes indeed … sometimes things are not all as they appear to be. You two must be very careful," he said with a look of concern on his face.

'Oh my, he knows the truth of it! The fairies have always

been able to see through to the truth of things,' thought Piffels to himself as a wave of unease washed over him. Just then Master Evergreen and Myra Silverstone walked up to them.

"Ebermarl, my old friend, how have you been ... it has been a long time," said Master Evergreen with a warm smile as he grasped the fairy's hands in greeting.

"Evergreen, my old friend, all is well; I was just getting to know this delightful, if a bit unique, little lady elf. And who is this lovely lady elf with you?" he said as he looked carefully at Myra.

"This is Myra Silverstone, the Daemon of Dundeen. She is visiting on her way to another village. Twinkles is her granddaughter."

"The Daemon of Dundeen; well then, I am honored to meet you both. I have visited Dundeen, a lovely village," said Ebermarl as he continued to carefully look and walk around both Twinkles and Myra.

"Yes - well all good things must start somewhere, and most great things do not happen without some risk," said Master Evergreen with a wink and a nod.

"You are right as always, my old friend ... see you again soon," said Ebermarl as he flexed his wings, leaped upward, and flew off toward the distant forest. All four of them watched as Ebermarl quickly disappeared into the blue sky.

"Fairies are fascinating creatures," said Master Evergreen. "Piffels...would you fetch the cart? The day is young and there is much yet for Twinkles to see."

Chapter Five

Greenbriar Village

The center of Greenbrier Village was just a short cart ride on a dirt road from the Greenbrier Emporium. After rounding a small hill, the village of Greenbrier came into view. Clustered around a large village square was a sizeable stand of tall white daisies and golden yellow marigold flowers. Their interlocking flower petals and leaves looked a lot like a colorful forest canopy. Twenty small single story white cottages that looked a lot like little mushrooms were interspaced between the tall flower stalks. Each cottage was made of vertical poles around which were woven vines and grasses. A layer of a white plaster-like material was smoothed over the vines and grasses, giving each cottage a whitewashed appearance. Some of the cottages had roofs made of interlocking pinecone scales, much like shingles, and some of the cottages used grass thatching for their roofs. Each of the cottages was fitted with several windows covered by transparent sheets of mica. Little curls of smoke from a few of the cottage chimneys created a slight gray haze over the entire scene. Elves always take great pride in dressing up their living spaces with brightly painted wooden windmills and whirligigs of all shapes and sizes that dance and move in the smallest breeze. Each cottage was connected to the village square by a stone path. A large fountain, a pool of water, and a gazebo-like building dominated the center of the village square. Elves of all ages were moving to and fro between the cottages and the village square, and mice-drawn carts carrying all manner of things were moving between the village and the surrounding countryside. The swaying of the flowers in the breeze and the motion of the colorful windmills and whirligigs gave a festive appearance to the village. Way off in the distance, barely to be seen, was the Daemon's Observatory on top of Gobstop Hill.

"This looks like such a wonderful, happy place," said Twinkles, giggling and clapping her hands.

"Yes - it is indeed a very happy place," said Piffels, as warm memories of his childhood in the village washed through his mind.

Master Evergreen drove the cart to the outside edge of the village. Several other carts and their mouse teams were tied up to a large hitching pole driven into the ground. After tying up the two mice and the cart to the hitching pole, everyone got out of the cart and began walking into the village. As they entered the village square, an older male elf recognized Master Evergreen and walked over to them.

"Master Evergreen, to what do who owe the honor of your visit to our village?" asked the older male elf as he grasped Master Evergreen's hands.

"Pudgkin, my old friend, it has indeed been too long since my last visit. I have with me some visitors. Mrya Silverstone, the Daemon of Dundeen, and her young charge, Twinkles Pink Blossom."

"Welcome to Greenbrier Village. New friends are always welcome here," said Pudgkin, smiling and grasping the hands of both Mrya and Twinkles. "Twinkles, I think there are some young elves in the village who would very much like to meet you."

"Piffels, you and Twinkles go on and have some fun in the village. We will meet you at the fountain at quarter past full sun. It is full sun now, so you will have some time with your friends," said Master Evergreen.

"Piffels is back, Piffels is back!" exclaimed an excited young elf as he ran from cottage to cottage making the announcement. It seemed that being the Daemon's apprentice made him a young elf of some importance and of significant pride for the village. Before too long Piffels and Twinkles were surrounded by a small crowd of excited young elves all clamoring to hear about his adventures with the Daemon and curious about the new visitor, Twinkles Pink Blossom.

"Piddles, Twaddles, Gemmalinka, Marigold and Gimlinka, good friends all; it is so good to see you all again. I want to introduce you to my good friend Twinkles Pink Blossom from village Dundeen."

"Hello and welcome Twinkles. From village Dundeen, eh? Well swizzles, you are a long way from home," said Piddles, bowing and doffing his little cap.

Twaddles muscled in front of Piddles and said, "My name is Twaddles and I am the fastest runner in the village. It is more than a wonderful pleasure to meet you."

Gimlinka, being taller than the rest, pushed both Piddles and Twaddles aside. "My name is Gimlinka and I am the strongest elf in the village," he said as he pulled himself up to appear even taller.

"Oh poo, you are all glomsquach!" exclaimed Marigold as she stepped between Gimlinka and Twinkles. Putting her arm around Twinkles and glaring at Gomlinka she said, "Come and sit with us. We don't need a bunch of worthless flirts." Gomlinka stuck out his tongue at Marigold but stepped aside.

Twinkles smiled at being the center of so much attention, but also felt strangely uncomfortable knowing that she was in disguise. She said, "Thank you for all your kindness, I think you are all wonderful friends. I know Piffels wants to share his adventures as the Daemon's apprentice and then I would like to see your village."

Everyone gathered around Piffels as he began to tell of his work in the Daemon's observatory. While he shared every detail of his many adventures, he was very careful to leave out his adventure outside the great stonewalls. Everyone hung on his words, with many questions being asked about his work as the Daemon's apprentice.

The village was a fascinating place for Twinkles. With the girl elves Gemmalinka and Marigold as her guides, Twinkles was given a complete tour of the village. The Village Square was paved with smooth stones that reminded

Twinkles of the pictures of cobblestone streets that she had seen in some of the books at her school. At the very center of the square was a large pool of water. In the center of the pool was a small fountain from which water cascaded into, making a pleasant tinkling sound. It was explained by Gemmalinka that each morning elves would come from their cottages with large ceramic jugs to fill from the pool, as there was no running water in the village. A small stream flowed next to the village that served to both wash clothes and for bathing.

In the front of each of the cottages was a collection of wooden windmills and whirligigs, all brightly painted. It seemed to Twinkles that each family was trying to outdo all the others with these mechanical displays. Inside, the floors and walls were coated with the same hard white coating that was on the outside of the cottages. Each elfin family took pride in painting the walls bright colors to give the inside a bright, cheery feeling. All the furniture was rather simple and largely made by hand. One room in each cottage was designated the kitchen. A large fireplace with a big metal pot on a hook dominated that area. Several other rooms were for sleeping, and the largest room was set with a large table and chairs as a living room. Twinkles found the cottages very comfortable and enjoyed the company of her new friends.

"Where do you go to school?" Twinkles asked Marigold, who appeared to be a little bit little older than Gemmalinka.

"What is school?"

Twinkles thought about Marigold's response for a minute and then said, "In my own village there is a place we call school where young elves go to learn about the world."

For the first time, Marigold looked at Twinkles a bit differently and thought to herself, 'Hmmm, school eh? … Dundeen must be a very different village and … there is something odd about this little elf. I can't quite put my finger on just what is odd but odd it is. Nevertheless, I do like Twinkles a lot and no matter what, I will call her a good friend.'

"Oh yes, the Elder Ones, they come every four full suns to share stories about the world. We all meet in the village square … it's quite a lot of fun," said Marigold.

Twinkles thought about how different her own home humankind world was from this elfin world and how it would be to not have to go to a place called school. Soon enough, the sun was very low on the horizon when Piffels finally caught up to Twinkles and her guides.

"Twinkles! We have to go! It is well past three quarter sun and Master Evergreen will have my hide!" said Piffels, all out of breath.

There were hugs all around and kisses of friendship. It is an elfin custom for two elves, male or female, to kiss each other to seal a friendship. Twinkles promised that she would see Marigold and all her new elfin friends very soon. Little did Twinkles know just how prophetic a statement that was!

Piffels and Twinkles made their way to the center of the Village Square and saw that Master Evergreen and Mrya Silverstone were waiting for them. Master Evergreen had his hands on his hips and an angry look on his face. Piffels thought about all the particularly unpleasant punishments that he had suffered in the past for various infractions of the rules, and wondered to himself just which one was in store for him this time.

"Where have you two been? We have been worried sick about you. Is Twinkles all right?"

"I'm sorry for being late, but we were so busy helping Twinkles learn about our ways and making friends that we lost track of time. It won't happen again," said Piffels, lowering his head a bit as he spoke.

"See to it that it does not!" Then a smile appeared on Master Evergreen's face and his expression changed to that of a proud father. "I am proud of you both," he said, looking at Twinkles with a wink.

"I trust that you are finding elves to be as warm and fascinating as I have over the years," said Myra Silverstone to her granddaughter.

"I do love it here, it's so happy, warm and loving, and Piffels is a wonderful friend," said Twinkles with a smile.

Piffels looked at the ground, blushed and shuffled his feet. "I too have found a wonderful friend," he said as he blushed again.

"The land of the elves is a wonderful, happy place as you have seen, but be aware that there is a dark side in the land of the elves as well. But there is ample time to talk of that later. Right now we are in need of haste as we are late for our arrival at the farm," said Master Evergreen. He led the party to the outside edge of the village.

Twinkles was not sure what Master Evergreen meant by the dark side of the elves. She found everything here to be so happy and loving that it was difficult to think that anything about elves could be dark. She promised herself to ask her grandmother about that when she had the chance. Right now was the excitement of the cart ride to Piffels' home, the farm where he grew up. Piffels had told her some things about the farm and about the time when he was but a wee bobbin, and she was very eager to see it for herself.

Chapter Six

Thistle Seed Farm

Twinkles guessed it to be about a half hour cart ride from the village to the surrounding countryside and the small cottage and barn like building that marked Thistle Seed farm. A small sign alongside the road marked the entrance to the long drive up to the farm cottage. Where the cottages of the village were rather small, the cottage at Thistle Seed Farm was very large, looking much like three small cottages pieced together.

The sun had set and it was dark outside when they pulled the cart up to the front door of the farm cottage. Warm yellow light spilled from the mica-covered windows to light up the path, creating a warm, welcoming scene. A small, round, gray-haired female elf opened the front door and the delicious smells of fresh cooked food followed her outside.

"Elron, so glad you are all right. It was getting late and we were a bit worried," said the gray haired lady elf.

"Mondra, you look as lovely as ever," said Master Evergreen as he stepped down from the cart. "Where is that husband of yours?"

"Sal and the bobbins are just coming in from the fields. We have been harvesting mustard seed and dill seed all day. Looks to be a good crop this year," said Mondra as she looked up to see Piffels and two other elves stepping down from the cart. "Piffels my boy! Come here and let me look at you. Has it has been two seasons already since I last looked upon you? Elron, it looks like you are feeding him well."

Piffels wrapped his mother in a large warm hug and a planted a kiss on her cheek. "It has been too long; it is so nice to be home once again. Let me introduce two new friends, Myra Silverstone, the Daemon of Dundeen, and her granddaughter, Twinkles Pink Blossom."

Mondra grasped Myra's hands in elfin greeting and said, "The Daemon of Dundeen, we are indeed honored. Welcome to our humble home. Twinkles, what a lovely name for a lovely little elf. Welcome, Twinkles," said Mondra as she grasped Twinkles' hands.

"Do come in out of the chilly evening air, and make yourselves at home," said Mondra as she ushered everyone inside and closed the cottage front door. The inside was painted a warm yellow color which reflected the warm yellow light from the candle lamps on the table, giving the inside the feeling of a warm summer day. Hand made chairs fitted with hand decorated cushions were set around a large wooden table. Wooden bowls and spoons were set in a circle on the table. A large fireplace dominated the far wall. Several large kettles were suspended from swinging hooks set next to the flames from a large fire in the fireplace. The kettles were the source of the delicious food aromas. Just then four roughly dressed elves, all smelling strongly of mustard and dill seed, walked into the room from a rear door.

"I see we have guests. Elron you wily old elf, how have you been?" said the older male elf.

"Sal, my old friend, it smells like the seed crop is a good one!" said Master Evergreen with a smile, grasping Sal's hands in a warm greeting.

"Piffels! My boy, it is good to see you," said Sal as Piffels wrapped his father in a warm hug and kissed him on the cheek. "You must tell me all about your training and the observatory ... who are these lovely lady elves?"

"Father, let me introduce Myra Silverstone, the Daemon of Dundeen, and her granddaughter, Twinkles Pink Blossom. Myra and Twinkles, this is my father, Sal Rose Blossom, Squire of Thistle Seed Farm," said Piffels with a little bow.

Piffels turned to the side and stood next to three young male elves. "These are my brothers still at home, Twiddles, Twaddles, and Fiddles," he said, pointing to each one in turn. Each of the boy elves smiled and waved at Twinkles.

"Alright then, Sal, boys, go wash up, supper is ready. Everyone come have a seat at our table," said Mondra, placing several platters loaded with steaming, sweet smelling food on the table. On one platter was a roasted grub surrounded by cooked mustard greens, and the other platter was a variety of roasted vegetables and seeds. A third platter was loaded with home-baked bread, and ceramic mugs were placed on the table. A large pitcher of water completed the meal setting.

Bowls were passed as Sal loaded each one with selections from each platter. After all were served, Sal sat back down and asked everyone to bow his or her head as he gave the meal blessing. "We give thanks to Gaia, the bringer of all goodness, for this bounty we are about to enjoy."

Everyone began to eat with small talk circulating about the table. Twinkles took a bite of the roasted grub and said, "Yummy! This tastes just like chicken." Everyone stopped talking, and Sal asked, "What is chicken?"

Master Evergreen, seeing the look of panic on Twinkles' face, smiled and said, "Chicken is a rare fairy delicacy usually only consumed on special occasions."

Sal laughed and said to his wife, "Mondra dear, I know you are a good cook, but to have roast grub compared to a rare fairy delicacy, now that is something." He laughed and slapped his leg. Mondra smiled, never having had her cooking so honored before. The chatter about the table picked up again as the meal continued.

Esmeralda would later write in her diary that never had she eaten food so savory and delicious. It was even better than her favorite fried chicken and smashed potatoes that her mother cooked. Not only was the meal enjoyable, but she also she felt so at home with this humble family of farmer elves - these elfin folk who were so full of love.

After the meal was finished and all was cleaned up, everyone sat around the fireplace. Sal played music on a homemade flute and everyone sang elfin songs. On several occasions Piffels and his brothers danced a happy elfin jig as everyone clapped. Twinkles found herself totally captivated and swept away in the joy and happiness of it all. Piffels, his three brothers and Twinkles engaged themselves in an elfin version of pick-up-sticks as Sal and Master Evergreen sat back and lit their pipes, the smoke hanging like a happy haze in the fireplace lit room.

"Sal, what crops do you harvest here on the farm?" asked Myra.

Sal puffed on his pipe and leaned forward a bit and said, "We harvest a variety of seeds, primarily mustard and dill seed, and a host of flower petals. We use the plant stalks as firewood and building material. Grubs, moths, beetles and occasionally mouse provide the meat sources for our diet." He puffed again on his pipe and continued, "Most of the seed we take to market at the Emporium; the rest we use here on the farm." Sal drew a diagram of the farm on a sheet of paper and pointed out the various crop areas. "This season has been a good one with a large crop of both mustard and dill seed."

"So Myra, what brings you to our little corner of the world?" asked Mondra.

"We are on a journey to another village and decided to stop and visit my old friend and fellow Daemon, Elron Evergreen. And I thought it a good education for my granddaughter Twinkles to accompany me on the journey," said Myra Silverstone.

"Well it is an honor to know you," said Sal with a smile. "And now Piffels, tell us of your adventures."

Piffels talked well into the night about his training as Daemon and all the fascinating observations he had made at the observatory. Everyone listened intently, absorbing every detail. Of course Piffels was very careful to not mention his adventure outside the great stonewalls.

All too soon it was time for sleep. Myra and Twinkles were given a room to themselves and Piffels slept with his brothers. Once inside their room with the door locked, Twinkles was glad to take off the wig and lay down on the soft down bed. Her grandmother pulled up the coverlet to her chin and kissed her granddaughter on the forehead.

"Sleep well, Twinkles. I love you."

Twinkles was so very tired and sleepy. It had been a long and exciting day. Tomorrow she would begin her journey back to her own home. She dropped off to sleep while visions of elves and fairies danced in her mind.

Chapter Seven

Journey Home

Just as the sun rose over the horizon, Myra Silverstone heard a knock on the bedroom door. "Good morning … the morning meal is ready," said Mondra.

"We are awake and will be right there," Myra replied through the closed door.

"Twinkles, time to get up," said Myra as she gently shook her granddaughter.

After washing up in the little basin in the room, Myra helped Twinkles with the elfin wig and adjusted her skin coloring a bit. On a table next to the beds was a small jar containing rose water that they sprinkled on themselves.

"Oh, this smells so pretty," said Twinkles

The large wooden table in the center of the cottage was set with wooden bowls and several large platters loaded with hot, sweet smelling food. Each bowl was filled to the brim with steaming hot pumpkin seed porridge. Piffels and his brothers were already busily dipping slabs of home baked bread in the porridge.

Piffels looked up to see Twinkles sitting down at the table, and said, "Good morning Twinkles, did you sleep well?"

"I did sleep very well, thank you," Twinkles said, as she busied herself with spoonfuls of rich savory pumpkin seed porridge and bites of warm, homemade bread. She found it both sweet and spicy. There was fried grub, sweet and juicy, roasted dill root with mustard seed sauce, and other wonderful, rich and spicy foods. Twinkles tried to taste them all and soon found herself quite full.

"Piffels, Twiddles and Twaddles, make sure that the mouse team is fed and watered and hitch them up to the cart. There is a long cart ride ahead for our guests," said Sal as he pushed himself away from the table. "Mondra dear, a wonderful morning meal as usual," he said as he kissed his wife.

Twinkles walked over to Sal and Mondra and grasped each of their hands. "I want to thank you both for your wonderful hospitality and kindness. I have enjoyed myself."

"It was our pleasure, and may the blessings of Gaia be with you as you continue your journey," said Mondra with a smile and a kiss on Twinkles cheek.

"May happiness and joy be yours always," said Sal as he too kissed Twinkles on the cheek.

"Everyone into the cart, we have a long way to go today,"

said Master Evergreen, standing in the open doorway to the cottage.

Twinkles stepped outside to a site that took her breath away. Arrayed before her were vast open fields with stands of tall dill, and mustard seed plants looking for the entire world like dense patches of forest. Piles of cut plant stalks dotted the fields like so many brown mushrooms. Several brown mice milled about inside a large fenced area. The white farm cottage and the barn like building looked like gleaming white temples in the soft morning light. In a sheltered area next to the farm cottage, short lengths of cut plant stalks were stacked like cordwood. A low haze of light morning fog and a quiet hush hung over the entire scene that gave a magical, dreamy feeling to the landscape. The scent of raw mustard and dill seed hung heavy in the air. Twinkles just stood there in awe. Piffels came to her side, put his arm around her shoulders and said, "A wonderful awesome scene isn't it. I do miss it so much."

Twinkles looked at Piffels and saw a tiny tear streaming down his cheek. Twinkles could feel something change inside her - something wonderful that she did not yet understand.

"Come everyone, it is time to go," said Master Evergreen. He helped Twinkles up into the cart. After everyone was seated, he waved to Sal and Mondra as he urged the mouse team forward. As the cart lurched forward, Twinkles looked over her shoulder to see Sal and Mondra waving to them. She waved back to them as the cart quickly picked up speed. She noticed that Piffels was looking forward with a rather resolute look on his face. She took his hand in hers as they traveled down the dirt path.

ooooo

The sun was already well above the horizon as they passed other farms on the little dirt road. Piffels described each farm as it came into view. First there was Hollyhock Blossom farm, a somewhat larger operation than the farm where Piffels grew up. Huge stands of tall hollyhock stalks heavy with flowers surrounded the farm buildings. Piffels explained that the hollyhock blooms were used for both medicines and food. The large woody hollyhock stalks made excellent building material. Next was Squash Blossom farm. Here the fields were heavy with small squash and pumpkin plants. Twinkles remembered her mother using small pie pumpkins to make pumpkin pies, but these looked so huge. Then she remembered that she was now much smaller elf size so the pumpkins looked much larger. They passed many other farms where all sorts of seeds and plants were grown and harvested. Twinkles began to realize there was much more to the land of the elves than she first thought.

Just as they rounded a small hill, a river set in the center of a valley came into view. Twinkles recognized it as the stream that flowed through her grandmother's garden. Here, as she was the size of an elf, the small stream appeared to be a large river. Several groups of elves were working with wicker traps set in the river to catch small fish and other aquatic creatures.

"This is the river Elba and is named after Elba Star Flower, one of the most famous elves in our history. It was Elba, a warrior elf, who single handedly saved thousands of elves from a massacre during the dark times between humankind and the elves. As the story goes, he sacrificed himself to save many others. The river is named in his honor," said Master Evergreen.

"It is from the river that we elves get our fish and other foods from the water. You see the carts lined up at the river over there?" Piffels pointed to the edge of the river. "As fish and other water creatures are caught, they are dressed and sent immediately by mouse cart to the emporium."

Master Evergreen pulled the cart up to the edge of the river where a hitching post had been set into the ground.

"Piffels, tie up the mice to the post and make sure they get some water. We will rest here before we go on," said Master Evergreen as he helped Myra and Twinkles off the cart.

"Oh my, it does feel good to stretch my legs after sitting in the cart for most of morning," said Twinkles. She walked around the cart and looked upon a wondrous scene. Next to the elves fishing in the river, a thicket of grasses spread out into the distance. The interlocking blades of the grasses looked to Twinkles like green swords all pointing skyward and looked an awful lot like a green ocean, the breeze moving the blades in an undulating motion much like ocean waves. It looked dark and mysterious and it seemed to go on forever disappearing in a blue gray haze off in the distance.

"It looks beautiful, doesn't it," said Piffels sensing Twinkles' fascination. "We elves call it the Wild Place. It is a place of danger. Dragonflies and other meat-eating creatures haunt the wild place. Some elves have entered and have never been seen again."

"Where does that road go?" asked Twinkles pointing to a dirt road cut through the grass.

"If you look up river just a bit, you will see a wooden bridge that crosses it. That road leads to the bridge. On the other side of the bridge is the road to village Brandywine, some four days' journey by mouse cart over areas unprotected by fairy glamour," said Piffels, pointing to the bridge off in the distance. "Would you like to go see it?"

"Oh yes, it looks fascinating," said Twinkles, clapping her hands.

"Master Evergreen, Twinkles and I are going to see the Elba Bridge; we won't be gone long."

"Very well, but be wary Piffels, the Wild Place is not to be trifled with," said Master Evergreen.

Just then a wild commotion broke out among the elf fishermen next to the river, with elves yelling and running away in all directions. Up in the sky there appeared two huge dragonflies, darting and diving toward the elves.

"Quickly, under the cart everyone!" shouted Master Evergreen. They could hear a loud buzzing sound as the dragonflies hovered over the wicker traps in the river.

"Piffels, I'm scared!" cried Twinkles and clung to him, shaking with terror at the scene as one of the dragonflies darted down to the carts and extracted a fat fish. Then seemingly out of nowhere, they heard a whooshing noise as two bolts from elfin crossbows pierced the body of one of the dragonflies. They heard an awful shriek as it dropped to the ground, its wings broken and crumpled under its now still body. The remaining dragonfly immediately flew off and disappeared into the distance.

"It's all right; the danger is passed," said a deep male elf voice. A large muscular elf dressed in a red tunic, brown laced boots, and wearing leather and metal body armor appeared before them. His long dark hair was woven into a long braid down his back. A large sword was strapped to his side and he held a crossbow in his hand. A quiver holding several crossbow bolts was strung across his back. Two other elves, dressed in the same red tunics and armor, also appeared.

"The old folks will feast tonight," said one of the elves, slapping the other on the back. "I still say I could have taken it with one shot," said the other elf.

"Come on you two, let's get going while it's still warm," said the first elf. The three elves worked together to drag the dragonfly carcass to a cart and hoist it on board.

Master Evergreen crawled out from under the cart and helped everyone else out as well. He walked over to the elf with the crossbow, slapped him on the shoulder and said, "Still sharp of eye and strong of arm I see."

"Evergreen! I haven't seen you in so long. My word, you haven't changed a bit; still that same old craggy, wise face." The elf wrapped his arms around Master Evergreen in a warm hug and then grasped his hands in elfin friendship.

"Star Fire, it is good to see warriors in action. And it so good to see you, my friend," said Master Evergreen.

"We are here to serve. The dragonflies and praying mantis have been more bold than usual, so we have been busy."

"How is your brother, Storm Singer?" asked Master Evergreen.

"He was taken in a battle with some praying mantis a season ago. But he passed bravely and I am proud of him; his spirit lives with me always."

Master Evergreen placed his hand on the warrior elf's shoulder and said, "I am sorry for your loss. I know how proud you are of him, as we are all are grateful for his service and sacrifice. The blessings of Gaia are upon you and your family, my friend."

"Thank you, and may your journey be a safe and happy one. Farewell, my friend," Star Fire said. He turned and joined the other two warrior elves on the cart and they drove off down the road.

Master Evergreen walked over to the elves at the fish traps and arranged for the purchase of a fine fat minnow to cook for the night's supper. The fish was carefully wrapped in leaves and given to Master Evergreen.

"It is time to be on our way," he said as he placed the wrapped fish in the bottom of the cart.

Everyone climbed back on board the cart. Urging the mouse team onward, they followed the road onto a high ridge that ran parallel to the Wild Place. Twinkles found it fascinating to see the sea of grass from this higher vantage point and were surprised by how different and small the Wild Place looked from above.

As the cart moved along the dirt road, Twinkles asked about the old ones that the warrior elf talked about. Master Evergreen explained that it was elfin custom that any creature harvested in the defense of self or others, was given to the old ones as nourishment for them as a gift to Gaia in honor of her abundance. In this way, the community is protected and those enfeebled by age are taken care of. Thus balance and harmony is maintained.

"Roasted dragonfly, now that is a delicacy that has to be eaten to be appreciated; I have had the pleasure of that taste on several occasions," said Piffels.

Twinkles shuddered a bit and made a face at the thought of roasted dragonfly, although she did remember that roasted grub actually tasted quite good.

Master Evergreen, noticing Twinkles' apparent disdain for the idea of a roasted insect, winked at her and said, "And you know roasted dragonfly really does taste just like chicken." Everyone laughed, especially Twinkles.

As the cart rolled on, Myra explained to Twinkles that from the Elba river onward was a wild untamed area in the elfin lands, and that the Daemon was the only elf this far out into the countryside. In order to accurately observe the natural world it was necessary to be isolated from other elves. Journeys such as the one they were just finishing did not occur very often and were much cherished.

The rhythmic motion of the mouse drawn cart lulled Piffels into a state of reverie. Happy thoughts of Twinkles and Myra, his newfound friends, washed over him like a warm wave. His life as a Daemon in training was a solitary and lonely one. It was so nice to spend time and have adventures with very good friends. He was sure that memories of this happy time would be with him for some time to come. He found himself happily breaking into song and inviting everyone to join him in some spirited elfin folk songs. Soon everyone was singing and clapping in rhythm. Master Evergreen joined in singing the bass parts, and everyone was having such a good time that they did not notice the passage of time and the sun dipping close to the horizon.

It was getting on to early evening as the cart rounded a small hill. Piffels looked up and excitedly pointed out the small rounded knob on the horizon that was just visible in the gathering twilight. He said, "Just there is Gobstop Hill and the observatory; that is our destination."

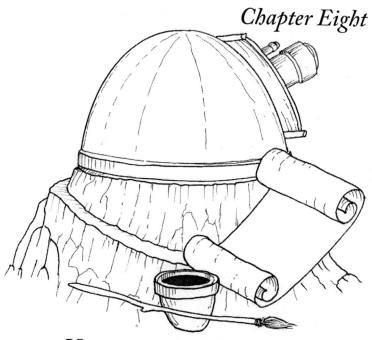

Chapter Eight

Home and the Observatory

Twinkles was very glad to finally be at the end of the long cart ride. It felt good to get down from the hard seat on the cart and walk around a bit. Master Evergreen's home was one of only four multi-story cottages in all of Greenbrier, the others being the homes of the village Elders next to the village square in Greenbrier Town. The white two-story cottage was surrounded by tall daisy and marigold flower stalks. The interlocking leaves and flower petals created a natural grotto that shaded the cottage from the rays of the sun. The white of the cottage walls contrasted with the dark green of the flower foliage and the light tan of the straw thatched roof. Twinkles thought to herself how beautiful and natural it all looked and how she felt strangely at home here.

"Master Evergreen, Twinkles and I are going up the hill to the observatory," said Piffels as he took Twinkles hand and started up the path.

"Very well, you will be called when the evening meal is ready," said Master Evergreen as he and Myra took the fish inside to have Esmenia prepare it for the evening meal.

The path to the observatory was a series of steps cut into the living rock of Gobstop Hill. A few lichens and mosses grew next to the path, but otherwise the area was devoid of vegetation. Twinkles was a little out of breath by the time they reached the summit of the hill. There in front of her was a round building capped with a gray colored dome. Piffels led the way to a small door in the base of the building. Once inside the observatory building they negotiated a set of spiral steps that took them to a second level. A truly amazing sight greeted her eyes. In the center of the floor was a large instrument that looked like a telescope. Shelves were arranged around the walls on which were fascinating looking instruments for observing the natural world. Piffels walked over to one side of the room and rotated a large crank. Twinkles could hear the dome begin to creak and groan as one side of it rotated inside the other to expose the room to the open air.

A fiery sunset filled the horizon and the stars were just beginning to become visible in the evening sky. Twinkles could just see the tiny firelights from the Town of Greenbrier. In the gathering darkness of the evening the tiny firelights looked to Twinkles as if hundreds of diamonds had been spread out on black velvet.

"Oh Piffels, it looks so beautiful."

"I know I never get tired of watching the sunset and the lights from Greenbrier."

"How come I can see stars, when you said that Fairy Glamour did not allow vision into the elf world?" asked Twinkles looking up at the star filled sky.

"Well that's because the Fairy Glamour shield allows natural light to penetrate, but does not allow humankind or the large animals of the humankind world to see into our world. Did you notice that during the day, the sky has a kind of silvery shimmer to it?"

"Yes, I guess you're right I did see that. I suppose I just didn't pay that much attention to it."

"The shimmer you saw was the Fairy Glamour. It's a sort of energy curtain created by the fairies to protect our world from the larger world outside. The great seeing glass in the center of this room..."

"You mean this big telescope?" said Twinkles, interrupting Piffels' explanation.

"Well ...We call it the great seeing glass but you can call it ... a ... a telescope. It allows us to see through the Fairy Glamour to the outside humankind world. Would you like to see your house?"

"You mean you can see my house in the humankind world?"

Even though the large instrument was very heavy, it was balanced so perfectly in it's mounting that Piffels could move it easily with one hand. He turned another crank at the edge of the room and the entire domed roof rotated sideways toward a dark area of the sky. Piffels moved a small stool under the instrument so Twinkles could reach the eye tube.

"Look through this opening and you will see your

house."

Twinkles clapped her hands with glee and stepped up to peer through the tubular opening. She let out a little squeal and said, "I can see it! I can see it, the back of my house. I even see my bedroom window. Oh wow!" She paused. "But why does it look like daytime at my house when it is night time here?"

"That is somewhat difficult to explain. You see, time itself moves at different rates in the different worlds. For example, one sun cycle, what you call a day, in our elf world would be the same as a very small part of a day in your humankind world."

Twinkles thought for a moment and then said, "So if I spent a day here in the elf world and then went back to my own world it would be as if I were gone for just a few minutes?"

"Uh huh, that's right," said Piffels as he rotated the cranks to close the observatory dome.

Piffels explained the purpose of each of the hand-held instruments arranged on the tables. One instrument, looking like a large protractor with a lever on it, was used to record the angle of the sun. Another that looked like a set of interlocking rings was used to record the position of stars. There was so many that Twinkles quite lost count of all of them.

"What are those strange looking symbols on the walls around the room?" asked Twinkles as she knelt down to examine one of them more closely.

"Those symbols are used to make the most important measurement of all. It is vital that the elves that work the land know when to plant and when to harvest. And others need to know when it is time for festivals and special ceremonies," said Piffels as he pulled down a thick heavy book from one of the many cupboards on the inside walls of the observatory. He opened the book and then continued, "I observe the position of the rising sun each morning and record it in the book. When the sun's position is aligned with one of the symbols, it means it is time for a specific elfin life event. At that time a message is sent to Greenbrier."

"Huh? A message, how do you do that?"

Piffels lifted a large device fitted with several shiny mirrors and said; "I use this instrument to direct flashes of sunlight to a specific place in Greenbrier Town. A young squire in the town has the job of using a small seeing glass to see the observatory at a specific time each morning. If he sees flashes of light then he knows a message is coming from the Daemon. The young squire has a smaller version of the mirror device to send flashes of sunlight back to the observatory. When I see that the squire is ready, I send the message."

"I see, but how do you send words using the light flashes?"

"Well I don't send words as such, but rather a set of numbered flashes. Each sun alignment has a number assigned to it. For example, when the sun is aligned with the symbol for spring, the time to plant and the beginning of the spring festival, five flashes of light are sent as the message. I send the five light flashes three times and wait for the flashes of light to come back from the Greenbrier squire telling me that the message was received," said Piffels as he demonstrated how the mirrors worked to direct the sunlight.

Twinkles saw how Piffels eyes lit up when he described all the interesting things in the observatory. The passion he felt for the task of Daemon radiated from him like a happy glow. She hoped that one day she too would feel as passionate about things in her own life.

Piffels stood facing Twinkles and took her hands in his, kissed her on the cheek and said, "This is how elves greet each other as friends. I would very much like to be your good friend."

Twinkles blushed. She kissed Piffels on the cheek and said, "I am your good friend as you are mine."

"Piffels, Twinkles, it is time for the evening meal," called Master Evergreen from the base of the spiral stairs.

ooooo

The evening meal was delicious. Esmenia had prepared a wonderful meal with the fish, roasted grub, and pumpkin seed soup. Twinkles was very surprised how cordial Esmenia was for the entire meal. Twinkles finally felt relaxed and as if she was really a part of the larger elfin family.

Master Evergreen invited everyone to sit in front of the fireplace and talk about the adventures of the day. This was a happy time with much laughter over mugs of hot raspberry leaf tea. Master Evergreen lit his pipe and soon wreathes of blue smoke hung around his head. The entire room had a delicious heady aroma that seemed to enhance the happiness and joy of all. Even Esmenia was smiling and laughing with everyone.

"This is the happiest day of my life," said Twinkles as she snuggled between Piffels and Myra Silver Stone.

"It is times like this that warm memories are made of, and it is those warm memories that sustain us when dark times come into our lives," said Master Evergreen as he leaned back in his chair and puffed on his pipe.

Twinkles thought to herself that with friends such as

these, how could dark times ever enter her life?

Piffels closed his eyes and thought about the adventures of the day and how wonderful it was to have such good friends. He promised himself that he would let nothing darken the lives of these good, wonderful friends. Little did Piffels know that there would very soon come a time when that promise would be put to the test.

"The hour is late and it is time for all good elves to sleep. Tomorrow is another day and we shall see what adventures await us all," said Master Evergreen as arose from his chair. "Twinkles, you and Myra will have the large upstairs bedroom. Everyone sleep well."

"Sleep well and pleasant dreams," said Piffels as he climbed the stairs to his small room. Twinkles and Myra followed up the stairs to the large bedroom. As they opened the door to the room they saw two wooden frame beds with down-filled pads and warm blankets woven from thistle and milkweed fluff that looked so good to a very tired Twinkles. Myra closed the door, and then both she and Twinkles removed their wigs and set them on the small dressing table next to the beds. Neither Twinkles nor Myra noticed the door to the room opening slightly or the pair of elfin eyes peering through the crack in the door. Nor did they see the door silently closing as they both crawled into the beds and fell fast asleep.

"I knew it! I knew there was just something not right about those two. Sickleswitch! Round ears, we are being invaded by round ears. I must see Raggles Chickweed about this immediately!" thought Esmenia to herself as she crept silently down the stairs. She grabbed her shoulder wrap and quietly opened the front door to the cottage and made her way to the cart.

Esmenia did not see Master Evergreen watching her from the shadows. 'And so it all begins; the prophecy is true,' Master Evergreen thought to himself as he recited the ancient prophecy: "Born of a great struggle, a round ear child shall lead them out of fear and into a bright new day."

"Many things to do; yes, many things," said Master Evergreen as he turned to enter his room.

ooooo

In her haste, Esmenia had only time to hitch one of the mice to the cart. Climbing aboard, she urged the mouse onward and sped off down the dirt road toward the cottage of Raggles Chickweed. It was a long drive by cart to the outskirts of Greenbrier, and in the quiet and coolness of the night Esmenia thought of all the stories of long ago, told by the Elfin Brotherhood about the ancient battles between humankind and the elves, and these thoughts only hardened her heart and resolve that soon it would be the elves who would prevail in the world.

Raggles Chickweed could not understand who would be knocking on his door at this late hour of the night. He crawled out of his warm bed, cursing under his breath, and opened the door. "Esmenia! You look a mess, come in out of the cold. What the squatch brings you out here in the dead of night?"

"Round ears, Raggles … round ears! We are being invaded by round ears!" exclaimed Esmenia.

"Make sense, woman! Have you been smoking snake weed again?"

"No! You fool! I have seen with my own eyes, not one, but two round ears disguised as elves in the company of Evergreen the Daemon," said Esmenia with a fire in her eyes and hands on her hips in a defiant pose.

"Evergreen, eh? The Daemon has powerful friends. I need proof and not just the ranting of an old Shaheena. I can't go to the Elfin Brotherhood without proof!"

"Proof! I will get you your proof!" said Esmenia as she wheeled about and stormed out the door. "You will have your proof," she yelled over her shoulder as she drove the mouse-drawn cart back down the dirt road.

The night air was the only thing that cooled the fiery embers of old hatreds that burned within Esmenia as she drove the cart through the night. Memories of the ancient stories of humankind cruelty toward the elves that the old ones had told her burned in her heart. 'Never again!' she thought to herself, 'Never again! There will come a time when it will be the elves that rule the world.' Esmenia's elfin ears burned with the spurning from Raggles. She had expected something entirely different from her friend and member of the Elfin Brotherhood.

Raggles Chickweed shut the front door and turned back towards his bed. 'This is not like Esmenia to have flights of fancy. She sounded more like some crazy old Shaheena. I must talk to the Elfin Brotherhood about this tomorrow,' he thought to himself as he crawled back into his bed and fell fast asleep.

ooooo

Esmenia arrived back at the home of Evergreen the Daemon just before sunrise. She unhitched the mouse and put the cart away, and then hurried into the house to begin preparing the morning meal. She was very tired, having ridden most of the night but she needed everything to appear normal to not arouse suspicion of the Round ears, Master Evergreen or that Sickleswitch Piffels. She busied herself, preparing the pumpkin seed porridge and vegetables and baking a fresh loaf of multi-seed bread. After setting out the bowls, spoons and drinking mugs, she walked up the stairs to knock on the bedroom doors, letting everyone know that the morning meal was ready. As she walked back down the stairs Esmenia thought to herself, "I will be a smiling and happy elf, yes I will ... but there will come a time, yes there will!"

Twinkles heard the knock on the bedroom door and Esmenia's voice announcing the morning meal. She stretched and sat up in her bed and thought about how nice it would be to be a real elf.

"Twinkles, I see you are awake," said Myra Silverstone as she pulled back the coverlet and swung her legs out to stand up. "There is a small basin with water on the little table. You go first and wash up and I will help you with your wig and clothing.

Both Twinkles and the older woman prepared for the morning, and then opened the bedroom door and walked downstairs to the kitchen.

"Good morning, you look hale and happy at the dawn of this fine day," said Piffels, using the classical elfin morning greeting and grasping Twinkles' hands in elfin friendship.

"Esmenia, the morning meal smells wonderful," said Myra Silverstone as they all seated themselves at the table. Just then, Master Evergreen appeared from the other room.

"Good morning, you all look hale and happy at the start of this fine day," he said as he grasped the hands of everyone in turn and then took his place at the table.

Everyone held hands as Master Evergreen gave the blessing for the morning meal. "May we all be eternally grateful and thankful to Gaia for life and all her bounty."

As soon as the blessing was finished everyone began eating. Piffels, always the one to be different, put his vegetables in his porridge and ate them together by scooping them up out of the bowl with a slice of bread. Twinkles found the porridge was good all by itself, and then folded some of the vegetables into a slice of bread and ate it as a sandwich of sorts. Whatever way the morning meal was eaten, it was not long before there were only a few crumbs and five empty bowls on the table.

"An outstanding morning meal; well done, Esmenia," said Master Evergreen as he arose from his chair. "Now it is time to help our guests on their way. Piffels, would you hitch the mouse team to the cart? Myra, Twinkles and I will meet you at the front door."

Piffels walked out to the little shed next to the house and moved the cart so that the mice could be hitched to the draw bar. While gathering the mice from the pen, he thought to himself about the coming sadness of having to say goodbye to his new friend. Even though she was humankind, she was so much like an elf. He felt strange new warmth inside himself when he held her image in his mind. He promised himself that this new friendship would not die, even though they were from different worlds, no matter what obstacles might get in the way. He remembered Master Evergreen's words – "Piffels, love can conquer anything." He smiled to himself at this thought as he hitched the mice to the cart.

Master Evergreen helped Myra and Twinkles into the cart and then climbed aboard himself. Esmenia stood in the doorway of the cottage, wiping her hands on her apron.

"Thank you, Esmenia for your hospitality. We have enjoyed our visit," said Myra Silverstone as she waved good-bye at Esmenia.

Esmenia smiled weakly and gave a little wave, and then went back inside the cottage and closed the door behind her.

Master Evergreen had a special secluded spot from which Myra and Twinkles could return to their humankind world. It was a quiet cart ride through a forest of tall grasses and flower stems. Everyone seemed lost in his or her own thoughts. The only sounds were the rhythmic patterings of mice feet on the ground and the creaking of the cart as they traveled down the dirt road. At last the road ended in a small clearing in a forest of tall marigold flowers. It was shady and cool; the overarching flower petals and leaves created an almost cathedral-like setting. The sunlight filtering through the flower canopy made speckle patterns on the ground that moved as the wind moved the flowers. Master Evergreen helped Myra and Twinkles down from the cart. In the very middle of the clearing stood a white pedestal on which was perched a silver garden gazing ball.

"Are you ready to return to the humankind world?" asked Master Evergreen as he placed his hand on Twinkles' shoulder.

"I would like to say goodbye to my new dear friend Piffels first. Is that all right?"

"Yes, of course. Take all the time you wish," said Master Evergreen. He took Myra's hand and moved to the edge of the clearing, leaving Piffels and Twinkles alone in the center.

Twinkles grasped Piffels hands in elfin friendship and said, "I will miss you, Piffels." Then she kissed him on the cheek.

Piffels blushed and said, "We may be in separate worlds, but whenever you think of me and say my name I will hear you and I will speak to you within your mind. You will never be alone."

"Will I ever be able to visit you again here in the land of the elves?" asked Twinkles, with a single tear moving down her cheek.

"I don't know. But my heart tells me that you will and that we will have some great adventures," said Piffels. Little did Piffels know just how prophetic that statement would become.

Master Evergreen and Myra Silverstone looked at Piffels and Twinkles holding hands in elfin friendship. "Elron, do you remember being young and your first real friendship?"

Elron Evergreen smiled and said, "These are the times of which special memories are made. My heart tells me that we have not seen the last of Twinkles the elf."

"You are my best friend, Piffels, and I will never forget you," said Twinkles as she turned and walked to the edge of the clearing. "I am ready now," she said to Master Evergreen.

All four walked to the center of the clearing. Both Myra and Twinkles placed their hands on the silver gazing ball. Master Evergreen and Piffels stood opposite the two women and also placed their hands on the gazing ball. Master Evergreen intoned the words:

"Forces of the Universe, I, Elron Evergreen, an Elf True, send this friend on her way to her True Home."

Then Piffels repeated the chant:

"Forces of the Universe, I, Piffles Rose Blossom an Elf true, send this friend on her way to her True Home."

A pillar of sparkling light began to form around both Myra and Twinkles. Both Myra and Twinkles together intoned the words:

"Hurly Burly Wackity Woo
It is home for me and you.
By the Towers of Chrome
There is No Place like Home"

The pillar of sparkling light grew brighter and brighter, until Myra and Twinkles became a part of the light. A brilliant beam of light shot straight up into the sky and the elfin wigs and clothing crumpled to the ground as both Myra and Twinkles disappeared into the light. And then the light was gone, leaving Master Evergreen and Piffels alone in the clearing.

Piffels picked up the elfin wig and clothing that Twinkles wore and held them close to his body. With tears welling up in his eyes he said, "Master, why does it hurt so much in my heart?"

Master Evergreen put his hand on Piffels' shoulder, and with kindness and wisdom in his voice, said, "What you feel is the loss of what humankind calls love and what we elves call Loreen. The Loreen you feel will be with you always. Just keep the memory of your friend in your heart and the hurt will pass in time."

Piffels quietly cried, holding the wig and clothing close to him as they both climbed aboard the cart and began to journey back home. Master Evergreen put his arm around Piffels' shoulders as the cart made its way down the dirt road and the sun dipped below the horizon.

⬦⬦⬦⬦⬦

Beverly and Esmeralda felt the electric tingling and tickling feelings as the back garden of the Hathaway home materialized before them. Then it was all quiet. They found the clothing that they both were wearing before they left for the elfin lands, just a few moments before, lying on the ground at their feet. Quickly they put on the clothing and made their way back toward the house.

With tears streaming down her cheeks, Esmeralda said, "Granny, why does it hurt so much in my heart?"

Grandmother Beverly put her arms around Esmeralda's shoulders and said, "What you feel is sadness and longing for your friend Piffels the Elf. Just keep the memory of him in your heart and the hurt will pass in time."

"Remember Esmeralda, the adventures that we had in the land of the elves must remain our secret. Do you understand?" asked Grandmother Beverly as they walked up the path to the back door of the house.

"I understand … our secret," said Esmeralda as she put her finger to her lips.

"Well that was a quick trip to the garden, you two. You were only gone a few minutes," said Jane to her grandmother and daughter as they both walked in to the house.

Grandmother Beverly winked at Esmeralda and said, "Well, sometimes great adventures can be had in a very short time."

Esmeralda winked back at her grandmother and smiled. 'Yes for sure, many, many happy adventures,' she thought to herself.

The rest of the late summer was a blur of warm, happy days, and every evening just before going to sleep, she would think of her friend Piffels the Elf and call his name. Many were the happy adventures they had together in dreamtime.

Then one day toward the end of that late summer, everything changed.

∞∞∞

Jane, Grandmother Beverly and Esmeralda were all sitting around the kitchen table, talking about what a wonderful summer it had been so far. Esmeralda was sharing all the interesting adventures she had in the garden and with her friends in the neighborhood.

"I have had so much fun this summer. Granny and I even went to see the elves and I met a good friend named Piffels," said Esmeralda with excitement in her voice. She looked up to see the scowl on her grandmother's face, and then realized that what was to have been a secret was a secret no longer.

"What is this elf nonsense? I thought I told you that there was to be no more of this evil in my house, and now I find that my daughter is living in a fantasy world!" Exclaimed Jane, her face red with rage. "I will NOT have this! I will NOT!"

"Now Jane, calm down, let me explain," said Grandmother Beverly.

"Calm down? Calm down! I will not calm down. I will not have my daughter's mind poisoned by your evil fantasies and imaginary friends!" Said Jane, slamming her fist on the table.

"But Piffels is not imaginary; he is a real elf and he is nice and he is my friend," said Esmeralda with tears welling up in her eyes.

"Shut up! I will deal with you later," said Jane, her face even redder than before.

Esmeralda was frozen with fear; she had never seen her mother this angry before.

"Jane! That is enough! Why do you find it necessary to

tear down everything that you do not understand?"

"It is evil and of the devil and I will not have it. I am going to send Esmeralda away to a boarding school where she will be a away from your evil influence."

Esmeralda sprung from her chair and ran out of the kitchen into the back garden. Tears were streaming down her cheeks. She felt as if her whole world was being torn apart.

"Esmeralda, come back here this instant!" shouted Jane after her daughter.

Esmeralda could only hear the wild beating of her own heart and the frantic calling of her friend's name, "Piffels, Piffels I need your help. Piffels, please help me!" She ran through the garden to the little clearing at the back. In a wild panic to return to the last place where she felt loved and happy, she placed her hands on the silver gazing ball and said, in a shaking sobbing voice, the magic chant:

"Whoosh, whoosh tingles
Sparkle in the Jingle
Poof, Poof Diffles
Make me just as small as Piffels"

The sound of tinkling bells, the strong smell of flowers and a tingling tickling feeling washed over her. The garden began to slowly disappear, to be replaced by a gray, misty fog. The mist quickly began to disappear as she found herself in Elron Evergreen's back garden surrounded by tall flower stems that looked like tree trunks, shrubs that looked like huge green swords sticking out in all directions, and several large and tall stones. Master Evergreen's cottage appeared out of the mist.

It did not feel the same. Esmeralda felt cold, and then realized that her clothing was left behind in the transfer to the land of the elves. There was no one to greet her, and suddenly she felt very afraid and very alone. She did not know what to do, so she called out Piffels' name.

Sometimes fate takes interesting turns, for just at that instant Esmenia was collecting seeds in the back garden. She looked up to see the little pink Round Ear wrapping a leaf around herself.

"At last, my proof has arrived, this is just what I need to convince that idiot Raggles Chickweed that the Round Ear invasion is real. Quickly she emptied her seed-collecting bag and ran up behind Esmeralda, throwing the bag over her head, trapping Esmeralda inside.

"Now I've got you, ya little glomsquach," said Esmenia as she wrapped the bag around Esmeralda.

'I must act quickly before that gleamsqueek Evergreen sees me,' thought Esmenia to herself.

Esmeralda screamed in terror and then her world went black. Esmenia hoisted the bag over her shoulder and ran up the hill to hitch two mice to the cart. She threw the bag with Esmeralda inside into the cart and quickly hitched the two mice to the cart drawbar. In the blink of an eye, Esmenia was urging the mice onward to Greenbrier Town.

ooooo

Piffels was in the observatory when he heard Esmeralda call his name in his mind, and then he heard a humankind voice call out his name in a scream of terror from the back garden. Piffels felt a cold chill down his back.

"Oh Ancient Ones … NO! My humankind friend is here and she needs my help," he said to himself. He ran down Gobstop Hill in a panic and burst through the front door of the cottage shouting, "Master, Master I need your help! Something terrible has happened!"

Master Evergreen came down the stairs from his studio and said, "What is it, Piffels? What's happened?"

"Esmeralda! … She is here! … And she is in trouble!" said Piffels, still trying to catch his breath.

"Are you sure? I have not heard from Beverly."

"I am sure of it … where is Esmenia? I saw her collecting seeds in the back garden," said Piffels with a new note of concern in his voice.

Master Evergreen closed his eyes, concentrated for a few seconds, and then said, "Quickly now, see if the cart is in the little shed."

Piffels did as he was told. He felt a chill down his spine as the discovered that the cart was gone and two of the four mice were also gone. He hurried back to the cottage and reported his observation to Master Evergreen.

"This is not like Esmenia to just leave without saying a word. Something unusual is going on," said Master Evergreen as he closed his eyes and stroked his beard. "Unusual indeed. I sense the Elfin Brotherhood is a part of this."

Just then Master Evergreen's eyes snapped open, his expression abruptly changed. "Beverly is coming; something terrible has happened with Esmeralda. Come Piffels, we must return to my study immediately. Just as Piffels and Master Evergreen entered the study, a shaft of sparkling light appeared and Grandmother Beverly stood before them. Master Evergreen quickly wrapped a robe around her and led her to a chair.

"Esmeralda has run away! There was an awful argument between her mother and myself. I think she has returned here to the land of the elves to be with you, Piffels," said Grandmother Beverly.

Piffels felt a cold sweat break out over his entire body.

He felt sick to his stomach and weak at the knees. He sat down in a chair and put his face in his hands.

"Piffels, what is wrong?" asked Master Evergreen.

"I fear Esmenia has already found Esmeralda and has taken her away, It's my entire fault. If only I were more alert," said Piffels as tears streamed down his cheeks.

Master Evergreen closed his eyes in concentration. "The Elfin Brotherhood. Esmenia has taken Esmeralda to the Brotherhood. She is in great danger!" said Master Evergreen.

ooooo

Esmenia drove the two mice as hard as she could down the dirt road to Greenbrier and the cottage of Raggles Chickweed. 'Raggles wanted proof; well, by the pillars of Renstraw I have the proof now!' she thought to herself as she stopped the cart in front of Raggles' cottage. She lifted the bag containing Esmeralda, hoisted it over her shoulder and pounded on the front door to the cottage.

"What is it? What is it?" said Raggles Chickweed, as he opened the door to see Esmenia carrying a large bag over her shoulder. "What the squatch is this?"

"You wanted proof, well I have your proof!" said Esmenia as she opened the bag, depositing a still unconscious Esmeralda on the floor of the cottage.

"A humankind child! Where did you find it?" asked Raggles as he bent down to better examine the still form on the cottage floor.

"That Gleamsqueek Evergreen has somehow opened a bridge between our world and the world of the round ears," said Esmenia with a satisfied, smug look on her face.

"Evergreen, eh! Well the Master of the Elfin Brotherhood will be very interested to hear what you have to say,

Esmenia. And they will be very interested in this human-kind child. We need to take care that she is not damaged," said Raggles while picking up the limp body of Esmeralda.

"It is a stinking round ear; I want nothing to do with it," said Esmenia

"Esmenia … No … This humankind child is an innocent and our guest. Now help me find some clothing for her to wear."

○○○○○

To Piffels, Master Evergreen's study somehow did not feel the same. Knowing that his dear humankind friend was in danger seemed to change everything. For the first time in his life, he felt truly lost.

"Beverly, what happened in your world that caused Esmeralda to return to the elfin world?" asked Master Evergreen.

"Esmeralda's mother Jane and I had an argument, and I think it frightened Esmeralda. This is a place where she felt safe and loved, and I think she wanted to feel that safety and love again," said Grandmother Beverly.

"This is my entire fault," said Piffels with his head bowed and hands over his face. "If I had not invited her into my world, she would be safe now."

Master Evergreen sat next to Piffels, put his arm around his shoulder and said, "We don't know that for sure, Piffels. Let me tell you of the ancient elfin prophecy … The Lattra Kree … It was written centuries ago by one of the wisest of the elves when elves and humankind parted. The prophecy said that there would come a time when a young elf would heal the wounds between worlds. I don't know if you are that young elf, Piffels; and I don't know for sure that this is the time, but let knowledge of the prophecy guide your actions."

"I understand, Master. I will try and remember all that you have told me," said Piffels as he stood up and started for the door. "Now, there is much that I need to do."

"Use care, Piffels; never act in haste or in anger," said Master Evergreen, rising from his chair to grasp Piffels' hands. "Let us pursue all diplomatic means to rescue Esmeralda. I sense that she is safe for now."

"I understand," said Piffels. He turned and walked out the front door of the cottage and ran up Gobstop Hill to the observatory.

Grandmother Beverly walked to Elron Evergreen's side, put her arm in his and said, "Do you really think that Esmeralda is all right?"

Master Evergreen stroked his beard and said, "I know the Elfin Brotherhood will not harm her. They will attempt to use her to destroy me and the other Daemon's. And they will fail."

∘∘∘∘∘

Esmeralda awoke to find herself in a small room. She recognized the elfin furnishings, and in a fuzzy haze her mind began to remember the frantic return to the land of the elves. She remembered arriving in the back garden of Master Evergreen and her feeling of being cold and alone and calling out for Piffels, but then everything went blank. Try as she could, she could not remember how she got here in this elfin cottage. The door of the room opened and a stocky male elf came in. He looked friendly and smiled at her.

"Well hello there, glad to see you are awake. My name is Raggles the Elder and you are a guest in my home," said

Raggles in his best rendition of the humankind tongue. "I see you look surprised that I speak your language. There are a few of us that have learned humankind language."

To Esmeralda his voice sounded kind of slick and oily, and it made her uncomfortable. "Where is my friend, Piffels?" asked Esmeralda, curling up with her arms around her legs.

"First things first; what is your name?" asked Raggles pulling up a chair opposite from Esmeralda. "I need to know your name so I can help you find your friend."

Esmeralda just pulled her legs up tighter and put her head on her knees. She did not know who this elf was or why she was here in this place. Her mother had always told her not to talk to strangers. She felt so alone and frightened. Where was her friend Piffels? Then she thought to herself that maybe this elf could help her find Piffels.

"Esmeralda, Esmeralda Hathaway is my name," she blurted out.

Raggles smiled an oily smile. "Esmeralda, now that is a nice name. Come with me, Esmeralda. I will take you to someone who can help find your friend Piffels."

Esmeralda thought for a moment, and then stood up and walked with Raggles the Elder out of the room. There was a cart already hitched with mice by the front door. Raggles helped Esmeralda up into the cart and then also climbed aboard.

"We are going to see the Master. He is one of the wisest of the elves. He will know how to find your friend Piffels," said Raggles as he picked up the reins and urged the mouse team forward. As the cart moved down the dirt road toward Greenbrier Town, Raggles asked Esmeralda, "So, Esmeralda, tell me about your humankind world."

ooooo

Piffels moved quickly once inside the observatory. He opened the dome and rotated it so he could see Greenbrier Town in the far distance. It was a clear day and the sun was shining brightly. He picked up the optical signaling device and began to send flashes of light toward Greenbrier. It was not the scheduled time for signaling and he hoped that someone in Greenbrier would see his flashes of light and respond. He signaled and signaled and saw nothing from Greenbrier. And then, just as he was about to give up, there it was, three tiny flashes of light, the response signal from his good friend, Frinkles. His heart raced as he quickly composed his message:

Urgent meet me at the fishmonger in the Emporium secrecy essential.

He waited for the response signal and confirmed that the message was sent back to him. Taking pen to hand, he composed a message on a sheet of parchment. He rolled up the parchment and put it inside his shirt. His mind was racing as he quickly closed the dome and raced down Gobstop Hill. He burst through the front door of the cottage and raced up the stairs to his room. He quickly strapped on his trusty sword and filled two pouches with food and water. Placing the pouches under his shirt, he raced back down the stairs and out to the mouse pen. Now elves use mice as draft animals to pull carts and plough fields. Mice are not normally ridden bareback, but these were desperate times. He quickly fitted a bridle on the fastest mouse of the two remaining in the pen - trusted Shadow Dancer, a black and white mouse. He swung his short legs up over the back of the mouse. Gripping the sides of the mouse tightly with his knees, he grabbed the reins and urged the mouse onward to Greenbrier at a fast gallop. It would be written in the chronicles many years later that never had a mouse run so fast. All he could think about was his friend Esmeralda in the clutches of the Elfin Brotherhood.

"Faster, Shadow Dancer, faster," he yelled at the mouse. He could feel a strange feeling of courage and strength rise up inside of him. It was the same feeling that he had when he first delivered his note to Esmeralda. Somehow he just knew that he would win the day!

Chapter Nine

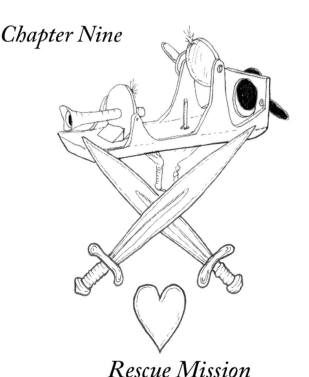

Rescue Mission

Arriving at the Greenbrier Emporium, Piffels tied up the mouse and ran inside. His good friend Frinkles was waiting for him at the fish merchant inside the Emporium.

"Piffels, what the squatch is going on? Why the urgent message? And why do you look like you have just had the mother of all mouse rides?" asked Frinkles with a look of concern on his face.

Piffels reached into his shirt and pulled out a sheet of parchment. "No time to explain; just know that many lives are at stake. Take this parchment and tell everyone on this list to meet me here in the Emporium, in one half sols.

Secrecy is all-important; let no one not on the list see this parchment. Can I depend on you, Frinkles?"

Frinkles unrolled the parchment and read the names written on it. "Some of these are warrior elves. It will not be easy to locate them," said Frinkles with a frown on his face.

"I know, I know, but speed is of the essence. Use the signaling drums if you have to. But they all must be here in one half sols. Frinkles, this is more urgent than you can imagine, now go!"

Frinkles rolled up the parchment and stuffed it into his shirt. "You can depend on me, Piffels," he said as he turned and ran out of the Emporium.

Piffels walked into the Emporium thinking to himself, 'I must find Sniffles and Snuffles; I will need their cunning and strength.' The two twin brothers, Sniffles and Snuffles, worked with their father in the metal working area of the Emporium. In the humankind world they would be known as blacksmiths. The brothers were unusually tall and broad of shoulder and were thought of by many as the strongest of the elves. The two brothers and Piffels grew up together and maintained their friendship over the years. Piffels could hear the rhythmic hammer blows on anvils long before the metal working area came into view.

"Sniffles … Sniffles, my old friend," shouted Piffels above the sound of the metal working.

Sniffles looked up from his anvil, and put down his hammer, wiped his hands on his leather apron and said, "Piffels, you little gleamsqueek, it has been far too long." With an ear-to-ear smile, he wrapped his beefy arms around Piffels in a huge hug and then grasped Piffels hands. "What brings you here, my friend?"

"I need the help of you and your brother with a great adventure," said Piffels with a serious look on his face.

"Your face tells me that this is an adventure of great importance and danger. Is this true my friend?"

"It is, and the time is short and the need urgent."

"Just a moment, I must talk to Macfest, my father."

After a few moments that seemed like an eternity to Piffels, Sniffles came back out from a curtained area with his brother, Snuffles and their father, Macfest, who was just as tall and beefy as his sons, only with gray hair pulled back in a long braid.

"Piffels, it is so good to see you. How is Master Evergreen?" said Macfest as he grasped Piffels' hands in greeting.

"Master Evergreen is well and I am learning much. You are looking well," said Piffels. "Now, I must speak with you about a matter of great urgency."

Piffels briefly explained the plan he had for the rescue of his friend from the Elfin Brotherhood, carefully omitting the identity of his friend as a humankind child. He explained that he needed the brothers Sniffles and Snuffles to assist him with security on the rescue mission. Macfest listened to Piffels' plan and said, "Anything that will bring the Brotherhood, may they rest in Gleemsqueeze, down a notch or two … I am with you in this." He put his hands on his sons' shoulders and said, "Make your father proud, my sons and …Piffels, make sure you bring them back to me."

Piffels grasped Macfest's hands and said, "You wish it, so it shall be."

Piffels and the two brothers walked back to the fish merchant area of the Emporium to find four elfin warriors and four young elves waiting for them.

The taller of the warrior elves said, "Piffels, what is this about a great adventure that can change elfin history?"

Piffels smiled to himself, for his friend Frinkles had followed his instructions to the letter. "Yes, that is true. Gather around, my friends, and hear what I have to share with you."

Now it was common knowledge in the land of the elves that the Elfin Brotherhood, for all its talk of the land of the elves for elves, was rife with corruption and criminal activity. It was no secret that the Master, as the leader of the Brotherhood was known, desired to disband the warrior elves and replace them with his own followers. It did not take a lot of convincing to secure the help of the warriors. All the while, Piffels was careful not to identify who it was that was being held by the Brotherhood. There would be time later to explain that his friend was in fact a young humankind female named Esmeralda. After he finished describing his rescue plan, Piffels said, "What say you, my friends, are you with me in this great adventure?"

Everyone looked at each other, and then one by one they placed their hands one atop the other, until all were arranged as the spokes on a wheel with their hands joined in the middle. Then, one by one they all said, "All for one and one for all, let the adventure begin!"

It was a long cart ride to the home of the Master of the Elfin Brotherhood where Esmeralda was being held captive. During the journey Piffels went over the plan with everyone. He alone would enter the front entrance. Two of the four warrior elves and the brothers, Sniffles and Snuffles, would remain just behind him but out of sight. One warrior elf and two of the four elves would move along the left flank of the house and the other warrior elf with the other two elves would move to the right flank of the house. They would occupy any guards or house security force. They had strict instructions to disable only, not to harm. Soon enough Piffels stopped the cart just outside of sight of the Master's house. There they waited, hidden from view, until the sun had just set below the horizon and the dim light of dusk encompassed the area. Under cover of the fading light, they advanced on to the house. Everyone assumed positions as Piffels, armed with his sword, opened the front door. While most elfin cottages had earthen floors, Piffels found himself in a long hallway paved with polished stone. The walls and ceiling were a uniform, featureless white. The hallway opened into a large room. There did not appear to be anyone at home. This place felt cold and empty, not warm and inviting as was the case with most elfin cottages. Piffels' heart sank. Was all this for nothing? Had they moved Esmeralda to a different place? Just then his old nemesis Raggles, son of Raggles Chickweed the elder, blocked his path.

"So ya little stinking pile of glomsquach, come to take my new gumdrop from me?" said Raggles with a sneer in his voice. "Piffels, the pet of that old fraud Evergreen, has come to take away my new prize. You are so pathetic."

Piffels could feel the sweat bead up on his forehead, his hands grew moist and he gripped the hilt of his sword even tighter. He remembered that Raggles had called Twinkles his "little gumdrop" in their encounter in the Greenbrier Emporium. He thought to himself, 'So Raggles you fool, Esmeralda is indeed here in this place.' There was a part of him, deep inside, that wanted to turn and run out the door. But just then he felt a wave of calm, self-assured courage rise up inside him. He squared his shoulders and stood just a little taller. He felt as if he could do anything he put his mind to. He chuckled quietly to himself with his new-found courage, and thought to himself, 'Yes Raggles, you are indeed a pathetic excuse for an elf.'

In a very calm and even voice, Piffels said, "Step aside Raggles, you are in my way."

"In your way! In your way! I'll show you who is in your way!" With a loud, screeching scream Raggles drew his sword, and holding it above his head, charged toward Piffels with anger and hatred in his eyes.

Piffels held his ground and remembered the words of Master Evergreen. "Use care, Piffels, and never act in haste or in anger."

Piffels braced himself with legs spread, sword held low but at the ready, and calmed his breathing. Raggles was running toward him now, screaming at the top of his voice, and then Raggles swung his sword with a slashing motion. Piffels deftly stepped to the side and flicked his sword upward, catching Raggles' weapon by the hilt and causing it to leave his hand and skitter and clatter across the stone floor. Raggles turned back toward Piffels with a look of total disbelief on his face. He picked up his sword and turned to again face Piffels.

With even more fire and hatred in his eyes, Raggles raised his sword to the ready and said, "You pathetic little gleezworm, I swear I will kill you where you stand."

Piffels stood his ground, legs apart and sword at the ready, and said in a calm, even voice, "I don't think so Raggles, for you see, my sword has not tasted elfin blood yet this day and it sings to me that it is thirsty. Do you wish to be the first to satisfy that thirst?"

Raggles stood still, as if frozen to the floor. This was not the Piffels he knew, not the little elf who would turn and run rather than fight, not the little elf he loved to torment. No, this was a very different Piffels. And for the first time in his life he felt the bitter, burning taste of fear. Raggles dropped his sword and then turned and bolted out of sight.

Piffels sheathed his sword and slowly walked down the long hallway, his footsteps echoing along the white walls and polished stone floor. At the end of the hallway was a large well-lit room. The walls of the room were lined with ancient tapestries illustrating the final battles between elfin and humankind. Like the hallway, the floor of the room was set with polished stone. The ceiling of the room was fitted with vaulted beams from which hung horizontal circular metal rings lined with lighted candles. In the very center of the room was a red velvet covered chair sitting on a slightly elevated platform.

Just then an unusually tall male elf with pink skin and ears, blond hair and blue eyes walked into the room with Esmeralda by the arm. She was wearing a long cloak with a hood covering her head and looked dazed, as if in a drugged state. Piffels had a heard many stories about the mysterious Master of the Elfin Brotherhood, but this was the first time that he had actually seen him, the last of the half breed elves, part humankind and part elf.

The Master clapped his hands and said in a sarcastic voice, "Very good, Piffels, I am impressed. Master Evergreen has taught you well. Now I assume you have come for this." He gestured toward Esmeralda.

Piffels started toward Esmeralda, but the Master held up his hand and said, "Wait, my impetuous elf, you are all alone and I have many who would come to my aid. It would be a shame for such a brave little elf to die so close to his friend." The Master clapped his hands three times and was greeted by silence. He clapped his hands three times again, and again was greeted by silence.

Piffels just smiled and cupped his hands to his mouth and sang out, "Kree, Kree, Kree."

Just then two cross-bow-armed warrior elves and the two elf brothers, Sniffles and Snuffles, both armed with stout wooden staffs, walked out from the hallway and alongside Piffels.

"As you can plainly see, you are wrong, just as you have been wrong about many things. It is you who are alone … Frankenflick … for that is your real name, is it not?" said Piffels in a calm even voice.

The Master sat back in his red velvet chair, and for the first time in his life felt genuine fear. He knew well of the prophecy, the Lattra Kree. Could it be that this little elf was the elf spoken of in the ancient prophecy? 'No matter', he thought to himself, 'this is but one small skirmish in the much bigger conflict to come.' He felt a new confidence that it would be he, the Master, who would be ultimately victorious.

Piffels called out, "Esmeralda, Esmeralda, it is me, Piffels, your friend. I have come for you."

Esmeralda slowly turned to face Piffels and raised her eyes. She blinked several times and then said, "Piffels, is that really you? They told me you were dead."

Piffels walked toward Esmeralda with arms outstretched and said, "It is really me; as you can see I am very much alive. I have come to take you home."

Tears welled up in Esmeralda's eyes and streamed down

her cheeks as she walked toward Piffels and into his arms. She put her head on his shoulder and softly sobbed. Choking back the tears, she said, "I want to go home."

The Master sat back in his red velvet chair and said with a sneer in his voice, "How very touching. You will see me again, Piffels. This is not finished."

Piffels turned his back toward the Master, and with Esmeralda and his friends at his side, they all walked out of the room.

As Piffels and his friends boarded the mouse cart for the trip back to Master Evergreen's home, Jurgles, the taller of the warrior elves, put his arm around Piffels' shoulder and said, "Never have I seen such bravery and brilliant tactics. Small you may be, Piffels, but you will always have a place with the warrior elves. It would be a high honor to serve with you ... but now I have a question. What is the strange language that your friend speaks?"

"It is a long, very complex story," said Piffels.

"Perhaps, but it is long journey back to the Daemon's home and we have plenty of time," said Jurgles.

And so it was that Piffels told his friends all about the humankind world and the ancient prophecy, the Lattra Kree, and all about the possibility of healing the rift between the worlds. Everyone listened intently as Esmeralda slept on Piffels' shoulder.

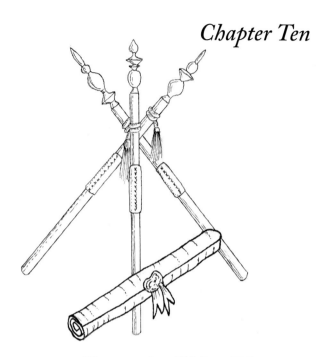

Chapter Ten

Summons From the Elder Elves

The morning dawned bright and sunny. Esmeralda awoke to find herself in a snug warm bed in the same room as her Grandmother Beverly.

"Where are we?' asked Esmeralda. She yawned and stretched and sat up at the edges of the bed.

"Well good morning, little one. We are in the home of Master Evergreen, the Daemon of Greenbrier. You have had quite the adventure, young lady," said Grandmother Beverly.

"Everything is all fuzzy...how did I get here?" said Esmeralda as she rubbed her eyes.

"You will remember in time, my child. Now it is time

that we freshen up and get dressed. I suspect our host is waiting for us."

A basin of water and fresh towels had been set out on a small table in a corner of the room. Fresh clean clothing for both Grandmother Beverly and Esmeralda was neatly folded next to the basin. After freshening up and dressing, both women left the room and walked downstairs to find both Master Evergreen and Piffels hard at work in the kitchen. As Esmenia was no longer in the employ of Master Evergreen, everyone pitched in to help fix the morning meal. Esmeralda noticed that Piffels looked different. She couldn't quite put her finger on what that difference was, but she liked what she saw.

"Good morning Esmeralda, you look well and rested," said Piffels.

"Thank you, I feel fine," said Esmeralda. She still felt confused as to why she was here in the land of the elves. She recognized Piffels, Master Evergreen and this kitchen, but it all looked different somehow. Piffels looked older and more confident than she remembered him. Having Grandmother Beverly and her friend Piffels by her side made her feel safe, so she decided to put the confusion out of her mind and help prepare the morning meal.

After a delicious meal of pumpkin seed porridge and home made bread, Master Evergreen asked Esmeralda, "Do you remember how you got here in the land of the elves?"

Esmeralda shook her head and said, "All I remember is that I needed to see Piffels, and then feeling very lost and afraid. The rest is a blur of confusing pictures." Esmeralda thought for a moment and then said, "I do remember a strange elf with pink skin and blue eyes, and I remember feeling very frightened."

Master Evergreen stroked his beard and said, "The Master, indeed. I fear we have not heard the last of old Frankenflick. Well you are safe now; your friend Piffels has seen to that."

Esmeralda got up from her chair and gave Piffels a big hug and a kiss on his cheek and said, "Thank you, Piffels, you are my best friend."

Piffels blushed, returned the hug, and said, "You are and shall always be my dearest friend."

Master Evergreen harrumphed and said, "Well now Esmeralda, you must always remember to contact one of us first BEFORE you journey to the land of the elves. For as you have seen, there is a dark side to the elves and we must all be very careful."

"I promise, and I will never forget to contact you first," said Esmeralda, nodding her head.

"Very well, now it is time for you to return to your humankind world. Perhaps there will be other times when you will again visit the land of the elves. Know that you are always welcome here," said Master Evergreen as he stood up from his chair.

Piffels placed his hand on Esmeralda's forehead and said, "I, Piffels, an elf true, bestow upon you the gift of elfin sight. Whenever the Moon is full and you think of me, I shall appear in your mind. You shall see my world through my eyes and I shall see your world through your eyes. Marloraca Maru Maru Shanaka KA!"

Esmeralda saw a bright flash of light in her mind and felt warmth on her forehead. She blinked, and then felt the gentle touch of Piffels in her mind.

Piffels stepped back, closed his eyes, and could feel the

gentle, warm touch of Esmeralda in his mind. Deep inside, Piffels knew that this was just the beginning of the adventure of a lifetime.

Esmeralda looked at Piffels with a smile, nodded her head and said, "Whenever the Moon is full we shall walk together."

After all was cleaned and tidied up, Piffels went outside to hitch two mice to the cart. Everyone boarded for the long ride to the special place that Master Evergreen had prepared for returning his humankind friends back to their own world. The trip went by very fast as everyone listened to Piffels recount his rescue of Esmeralda from the Master. Esmeralda in particular was clinging to Piffels' arm in rapt attention to every detail. Many questions did she have about what she did not remember, and with Piffels' help; many memories of that scary time began to filter back into her mind. Esmeralda felt so fortunate to have a friend true as Piffels the elf. Soon enough the cart stopped at the edge of a circular clearing in the grasses and flowers.

Esmeralda recognized the circular clearing and the silver gazing ball in the middle from her last visit to the land of the elves, and it brought back some warm memories.

All four walked to the center of the clearing. Esmeralda grasped Piffels' hands, looked into his eyes and said, "Upon the next full moon, look for me in your mind. I will be there." She leaned forward and kissed him on the cheek, and then turned to Master Evergreen and said, "I am ready to go home now."

Both Grandmother Beverly and Esmeralda placed their hands on the silver gazing ball. Master Evergreen and Piffels stood opposite the two women and also placed their hands on the gazing ball. Master Evergreen intoned the words:

"Forces of the universe, I, Elron Evergreen, an elf true,
send this friend on her way to her true home,"
Then Piffels repeated the chant:
" Forces of the universe, I, Piffels, an elf true,
send this dear friend on her way to her true home."
A pillar of sparkling light began to form around both
Grandmother Beverly and Esmeralda as they together in-
toned the words:

> "Hurly Burly Wackity Woo
> It is home for me and you.
> By the Towers of Chrome
> There is no place like home"

The pillar of sparkling light grew brighter and brighter
until they all became a part of it. A brilliant beam of light
shot straight up into the sky and both Grandmother Beverly and Esmeralda disappeared into it. Then the light was
gone, leaving Master Evergreen and Piffels alone in the
clearing.

"Master, it is strange, but I do not feel the same sense
of loneliness and loss as before. Is that because we have
bonded mind to mind?" asked Piffels as he climbed aboard
the cart.

"Very perceptive, Piffels, yes indeed, I think that not
only have you bonded mind to mind, but also heart to
heart, and that is a wonderful and rare thing. Cherish this,
son." Master Evergreen knew that the seeds of a true love
had been planted, but he would allow Piffels to discover
that for himself in the fullness of time.

In silence the two elves rode back to their home, each
deep in thought. Master Evergreen's thoughts were of the
Master Frankenflick and the mischief he knew would be

soon coming. Piffels' thoughts were of his friend Esmeralda. He thought about the wonders he knew he would see though her eyes. The adventure of a lifetime - that is what Master Evergreen called it. Indeed, Piffels thought to himself, an adventure beyond his wildest imagining.

ooooo

The sun was high in the morning sky when Grandmother Beverly and Esmeralda materialized in the back garden of the Hathaway house. The magical journey from the land of the elves heightened her senses, and Esmeralda noted how the air smelled differently and that there were birds singing. She had not noticed that there were no birds in the land of the elves. Her skin prickled with the cool, moist air in the secluded garden. Grandmother Beverly and Esmeralda quickly put on their clothing that had been lying in a crumpled heap by the gazing ball. As they both walked up the garden path to the house, they saw Esmeralda's mother Jane running toward them with her arms spread wide. She wrapped her arms around her daughter and said, "Esmeralda, thank God you are safe! Where did you find her?"

"She was in the back garden, all curled up and crying," said Grandmother Beverly.

"Oh Esmeralda, I don't want to send you away. I spoke in anger and in haste and I am so sorry. Please forgive me," said Jane with tears streaming down her cheeks.

"Momma, oh Momma ... I forgive you and I love you," said Esmeralda, her eyes welling up with tears.

All three women walked, with arms around each other, up the path and into the house. And so it was that late lazy summer that much happiness and joy was with the Hathaway household. Esmeralda was very careful not to mention her adventures with the elves to her mother. Sometimes in the early evening, Grandmother Beverly and Esmeralda would walk together outside in the gathering twilight and talk of elves, fairies and magic. On each full moon that summer, at night just before bed, Piffels and Esmeralda would walk and play together in their minds, each sharing a bit of their world with the other.

○○○○○

Upon arriving back at the Daemon's cottage, Piffels found the home empty and quiet, for Esmenia was no longer the housekeeper. Piffels felt strangely cold and empty. Even though he and Esmenia were never on the best of terms, he found that he missed her sharp tongue and presence in his life. He sighed and busied himself with tidying up the inside of the cottage. Then he and Master Evergreen worked together to prepare the evening meal. Even though the roast grub and pumpkin seed soup was the same, it somehow did not have the same flavor as when Esmenia did the cooking. He resigned himself to having to learn to do the domestic chores of washing clothes, cooking and cleaning. He gained a new appreciation of the role of female elves. And so it was in that lazy end of summer that Piffels lost himself in his observational duties and new domestic chores. He was happy and content. On his occasional trips to the Greenbrier Emporium he noticed that he was treated with a little more respect and deference. It was a new feeling for him that he found he enjoyed very much. In addition, Raggles and his crowd of malcontents were conspicuous by their absence.

On each full moon he would walk and play in his mind with his new friend Esmeralda. Many were the new wonders he saw through her eyes. The talking box with moving pictures that Esmeralda called a television fascinated him. The huge metal winged machines that carried people across long distances that Esmeralda called airplanes, he found particularly interesting. And then there was the four-wheeled cart that moved without being hitched to a mouse! Even the flush toilet was an engineering marvel that fascinated him. In the land of the elves, solid and liquid wastes were collected in soil pits. Every few months this accumulated waste was collected and used as fertilizer by the farmer elves. It was a puzzle to Piffels what the humankind farmers used as fertilizer for their crops. He promised himself that someday he would travel to the humankind world and see these wonders for himself.

Life had settled into a comfortable routine when one day in the early spring, the month of April by humankind reckoning, a message was delivered to Master Evergreen that would change everything. It was over the evening meal that Master Evergreen showed Piffels the message he had received. It was hand lettered in the formal elvish language and read:

> Greetings and salutations to Master Evergreen, Daemon of Greenbrier. Your urgent presence and that of your charge Piffels Rose Blossom of Greenbrier is required six sols hence to stand before the assembly of Elder Elves.

Piffels held the yellowed parchment in his hands and ran his fingers over the broken wax seal and asked, "What is the meaning of this message?"

Master Evergreen sat back in his chair, lit his pipe, took several puffs, and then said, "Piffels my son, this is a very serious summons. It is a very rare thing to have a Daemon stand before the assembly of Elder Elves. I sense that the hand of our old friend Frankenflick the Master behind all this."

"But why are we both being summoned?" asked Piffels.

Master Evergreen put down his pipe, got a very serious look on his face, and then said, "I believe it has something to do with your friend Esmeralda. As I have told you before, there are some in our elfin world who will stop at nothing to prevent the re-unification of the world of elves and the world of humankind. I believe they see the visit of Esmeralda to our world as a prelude to an invasion by the humankind world."

"But that is just wrong, crazy wrong!" said Piffels angrily.

"I agree Piffels, my son, but there are those who have only fear and hatred of humankind in their hearts, and some who feel this way are very powerful members of our own elfin society," said Master Evergreen with a heavy sigh. He picked up his pipe, re-lit it, and after taking several puffs continued; "Some of these same power hungry elves have always seen the Daemons as a threat to their quest for power and control. I fear that they see all this as a means to discredit all the Daemons and thrust our elfin world into darkness."

"Well, we must not allow them to have their way!" retorted Piffels forcefully.

"I agree, I agree," said Master Evergreen, smiling as he placed his hand on Piffels' shoulder. "Let us talk of strategy, about how to best pull the fangs of the Master and his minions."

ooooo

For many months Esmeralda had visited with Piffels in her mind every full moon, and it had become a happy, comfortable routine that she looked forward to each month. That spring, however, something happened that would change her world forever. On the full moon in April, when Esmeralda called out for Piffels as she had always done each full moon, she immediately sensed that something was wrong. Piffels was not his usual bubbly, exuberant self. A thin veil of gloom seemed to separate the two friends.

"What's wrong? Something feels very icky!" Esmeralda asked Piffels in her mind.

"There is big trouble here in the elf lands. The Master, may he rest in glomsquach, has brought charges of treason against Master Evergreen. I am really worried about all this," said Piffels with a quiver in his voice. Esmeralda could not see Piffels' face, but she imagined that there were tears on his cheeks.

"But why are these charges being brought? Master Evergreen is one of the most caring, loving elves I have ever known," said Esmeralda.

"I don't know, but Master Evergreen thinks it has something to do with your visit to the land of the elves. And he thinks that the Master is behind all this." Esmeralda felt a cold chill over her body at the mention of the Master. She did not remember everything from her time in captivity, but what she did remember brought her nightmarish dreams.

"Is there anything I can do to help?"

"I don't know of anything you can do right now. Talk to your Grandmother Beverly; she will tell you if there is something you can do. I must go now, my friend. I hope to see you again on the next full moon." Before Esmeralda could say anything, the image of her friend Piffels was gone from her mind. She felt a cold, sick feeling in the pit of her stomach. Tears welled up in her eyes at the thought of her dear Piffels in trouble.

"Grandmother, Grandmother!" shouted Esmeralda as she ran down the long hallway into her grandmother's room. She burst into the room and collapsed in a sobbing heap in her grandmother's lap.

"What is it, child? What's wrong?" said Grandmother Beverly, while stroking her granddaughter's hair.

"I met Piffels in my mind tonight, and there is something very wrong and icky in the land of the elves. Piffels and Master Evergreen are in trouble, Grandmother. Piffels had to go before I could find out what the trouble is. I feel so helpless. Isn't there a way that we can help them?"

"There, there child, I will speak with Master Evergreen about this. I'm sure everything will be all right. Let me fix you some warm milk and some cookies and then you need to go to sleep. I will check into this with Master Evergreen in the morning."

Later that night, after Esmeralda was fast asleep, Grandmother Beverly closed the door to her room and called to her dear friend, Elron Evergreen. When his image appeared in her mind she asked, "Elron, my dear friend, Esmeralda is in quite a fright from some trouble with you and Piffels. What is wrong?"

"Beverly, my dear friend, I need to see you as soon as possible. Piffels and I need your help with a matter most serious," said Elron with a worried note in his voice.

"As the sun rises here, I will journey to you and we shall talk of this serious matter. As the sun rises," said Grandmother Beverly.

Chapter Eleven

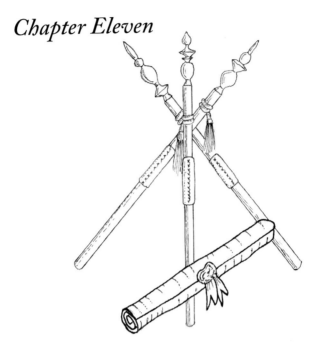

Council of the Elder Elves

It was a gray, overcast morning with a thin veil of fog that greeted Master Evergreen and Piffels as they hitched two mice to the cart for the day long journey to the Council of the Elder Elves in the village of Rosethorn. Piffels thought the gray day reflected his troubled mood very well. He had never been to the village of Rosethorn, and despite his worry and concern about appearing before the Council of Elder Elves, he found himself excited about seeing new places. Then there was the prospect of meeting the Daemon of the village of Rosethorn. Master Evergreen spoke glowingly about his dear old friend, Gaylord Flowerbloom. Piffels had heard about Master Flowerbloom's apprentice, a young man about his own age, and he was eager to meet him. The matter of his dear friend Esmeralda and her grandmother also weighed heavily on Piffels' mind. It was all arranged that the two humankind women would meet them at the home of Master Flowerbloom, the Daemon of Rosethorn. Piffels was worried for their safety, as he would not be there to greet his friend when they arrived from the humankind world. Master Evergreen had assured him that all precautions had been taken to ensure their safety. Even so, he still fretted about it as they climbed aboard the cart and set off on the journey.

"Piffels, let us go over the plan one more time," said Master Evergreen as the cart lurched forward down the road toward the village of Rosethorn.

ooooo

Esmeralda was playing in the back garden when she heard her grandmother call, "Esmeralda, Esmeralda, come into the house. I need to see you right away."

Hurrying into the house, Esmeralda hoped that there would be news about Piffels and Master Evergreen. Grandmother Beverly motioned her upstairs to her bedroom. Closing the bedroom door, Grandmother Beverly said, "I have news of the elves. Come sit down, child, there is much that you need to know."

Esmeralda sat down on the bed next to her grandmother and looked up at her with anxious anticipation. Grandmother Beverly looked down at her granddaughter and felt sadness inside, as she knew that the last shred of childlike innocence that Esmeralda felt about the elfin world was about to be shattered.

"Esmeralda, your friend Piffels and Master Evergreen have been accused of high treason against the elfin world.

They are to appear before the Council of The Elder Elves to answer to these charges that have been leveled against them. If the Council finds them truly guilty … high treason carries with it the penalty of death."

Esmeralda just sat there stunned, her mind reeling with the idea of her dearest friend being put to death. It was a few moments before she looked up at her grandmother and said, "What is high treason?"

"For centuries it has been unlawful for elves to make contact with the humankind world. By bringing you and me to their world, Piffels and Master Evergreen have broken one of the most sacred laws in the entire elfin world. There are some in the land of the elves who will stop at nothing to prevent the reunification of elves and humankind. You have already met one of them - he calls himself the Master. It is he who desires power above all else and who has brought the charges of high treason in an attempt to gain that power," said Grandmother Beverly as she handed Esmeralda a tissue for the tears that were flowing down her cheeks.

"But this is so unfair! He only wanted to be friends!" wailed Esmeralda as she put her head in her grandmother's lap and began sobbing.

Grandmother Beverly gently stroked her hair and said, "In all worlds there is both darkness and light. Right now, darkness has spoken. But all hope is not lost, for we are going to the land of the elves to help Piffels and Master Evergreen defend themselves and bring the light back to their world."

Esmeralda lifted her tear-streaked face and said, "We are really going to help?"

"Yes, my child. But there is little time and there is much

that I must tell you before we go. Are you ready to travel to the world of the elves to face an uncertain future?"

"Yes! I am ready. Tell me what I need to do," said Esmeralda, wiping her cheeks and blowing her nose.

"We cannot take anything from our own humankind world, so you must memorize much. Are you ready?" asked Grandmother Beverly

"I am ready. Tell me what I need to know," said Esmeralda.

∞∞∞∞∞

Piffels noted that the village of Rosethorn did not look all that much different from his own village of Greenbrier. The one big difference was the vast expanse of tall, wild rose brambles that surrounded the village. This being the early spring season, flowers were in full bloom and the heady scent of roses filled the air. In addition to the vast rose forests, the village of Rosethorn was famous for the beautiful furniture that elfin craftsman made from the woody stems of the roses. As their cart rolled past the Rosethorn Emporium, Piffles noted that it looked much like the Emporium in his own village of Greenbrier. The small homes were typical of most of the cottages you would find in most any elfin village. Then, as they rounded a small hill, the three-story building that housed the Council of the Elder Elves came into view. It was an imposing, awesome sight. It was built of all white stone. A long stone stairway led up to a front opening, framed by huge columns. It was like nothing that Piffels had ever seen. He suddenly felt very small, very small indeed. They continued on down the road to the home of Master Flowerbloom, Daemon of Rosethorn. The home looked very much like the two story home he lived in with Master Evergreen. The main difference was the huge three story stone cylinder attached to the side of the house. On the top of the cylinder was mounted an observatory dome. It looked very much the same as the observatory dome on top of Gobstop Hill back at his home in the village of Greenbrier. Piffels immediately felt at home here. A tall, older elf with white hair down to his shoulders and wearing a long blue robe was waiting for them as the cart came to a stop in front of the house. Standing next to the older elf was a much younger elf dressed in green pants and a brown shirt. Piffels guessed that this was Master Flowerbloom and his apprentice.

"Gaylord, my old friend, it is so good to see you. How many years has it been?" said Master Evergreen, grasping Gaylord's hands in greeting.

"Far too long Elron, far too long. You are looking well, my friend," said Gaylord, grasping Elron's hands in elfin greeting.

Master Flowerbloom put his arm around the younger elf and said, "This is Twiggles, my Daemon in training. And this must be Piffels," he said, grasping Piffels' hands in greeting.

"I am happy to meet you, Master Flowerbloom, and you too, Twiggles," said Piffels.

"Twiggles, I will show Master Evergreen and Piffels to their room. Will you take care of the mice and the cart? That's a good lad," said Master Flowerbloom.

The inside of the house looked very much the same as his own home with Master Evergreen. Upstairs in a small room they found two beds and a small storage chest. Master Flowerbloom put their bags on the chest and said, "This will be your room. My home is your home. When you are ready, come downstairs. There is much that we must speak of."

Piffels sat down on the bed. His bones ached from the long cart ride and he wanted so very much to just to lie down on the bed and sleep, but he knew that he needed to attend to more important matters first. He found himself worrying about his friend Esmeralda and wondering where she was.

"Piffels, find your writing paper and your pen. We must go downstairs and discuss our plans. There is no time to lose," said Master Evergreen.

Master Evergreen and Piffels walked downstairs to find Master Flowerbloom and Twiggles waiting for them. A large circular table had been set up in the sitting room. Six chairs were neatly arranged around the table.

"Piffels, before we get started, there is someone here of your acquaintance who would like to see you," said Master Flowerbloom. Just then from around a curtain appeared Esmeralda and Grandmother Beverly. Both Piffels and Esmeralda squealed with delight and ran into each other's arms. They danced around in a circle, hugging each other. Master Evergreen wrapped his arms around Grandmother Beverly and gave her a big hug.

"I think they like each other," said Twiggles with a smile.

"Indeed I think so too," said Master Flowerbloom with a chuckle.

Twiggles had seen many strange things as a Daemon in training, but elves hugging round ear humankind, now that was something he thought he would never see. He found these humankind females to be warm, loving, and not that much different than elves in his estimation.

All six then sat around the table and discussed strategy

for the upcoming appearance before the Council of the Elder Elves over warm mugs of tea and pumpkin seed scones. The candles had burned low and the night was almost gone before they all agreed that some sleep was well in order.

As Piffels lay his head on the pillow the events of the day were a blur in his mind, but the warm feeling of knowing that his dear friend Esmeralda was safe covered him like a warm blanket. Somehow he knew that great things would result from the events of the coming days. Feeling safe in that knowledge, blissful sleep overtook him.

ooooo

Just how incredibly important was this appearance before the Council of the Elder Elves was made apparent to Piffels by the appearance during the night of Daemons from all over the land of the elves. The villages of Poppyseed, Squashflower, Greenclover and several others Piffels did not recognize were all represented. It was very crowded that morning in Master Flowerbloom's drawing room. Piffels, Twiggles and several other Daemon apprentices were kept busy keeping track of carts and mice in the back garden.

Master Evergreen stood atop a small stool and rang a small bell to get everyone's attention. The chatter in the room quickly died down and everyone turned toward the sound of the bell.

"Thank you all for taking time from your own villages to offer your help and support. These are momentous times, my friends. The institution of the village Daemon is under attack from the Master and his followers. We must all stand together or we shall surely fall one by one to the forces of darkness. For as long as many of us can remember, we have yearned for reunion with the larger world. Because of the bold actions of a brave young elf, this dream is within our grasp. We must all be careful, as the Master's eyes are everywhere. You all know the plan. The humankind will go ahead with Master Flowerbloom and he will secretly deliver them to the Council chambers. We will follow a very short time later. May Gaia be with us as we go forth to make history."

A chorus of "So shall it be" echoed through the room, and everyone made ready for the short journey to the Council of the Elder Elves. Master Evergreen stepped outside into the back garden.

"Piffels, come with me. Twiggles and the others can handle the carts and mice. We have preparations to make.

ooooo

Esmeralda and Grandmother Beverly were both dressed in dark hooded cloaks as they climbed aboard the cart with Master Flowerbloom and Twiggles. The hoods were pulled up over their heads to hide their humankind identities. A feeling of both excitement and fear washed over Esmeralda as the cart began its journey to the Council of the Elder Elves. She knew that they were to be hidden in a back room and would appear in the council chambers at an appointed time. They were told not to worry that Piffels and Master Evergreen would be all right, and that they were all a part of an important history-making event in the lives of both elves and humankind. This knowledge was of little comfort to Esmeralda as she clung to her Grandmother and wished that she could be with her friend Piffels. It seemed as if only a few minutes had passed by when the cart pulled up at the rear of the Council building and they all quickly went inside to a small room. Twiggles was instructed to stay with them, and he did his best to make them feel comfortable and at ease.

Piffels felt very small as he walked up the long stone steps to the entrance of the Council of Elder Elves. As they approached the entrance, a large wooden door slowly swung open and they found themselves looking down a long hallway. Polished stone covered the floor of the hallway and the walls were a featureless snow white. Piffels was unnerved by the similarity of this hallway to the entrance of the Master's home. As they slowly walked down the long hallway their footsteps echoed along the walls. As they neared the end of the hallway they could hear a murmur of voices. It sounded a bit like the din of voices in the Greenbrier Emporium, only much louder and bigger. The hallway opened into a large enclosed arena. It was the largest enclosed space that Piffels had ever seen. The chamber was three stories tall with sloping seats that were arrayed from the floor to the ceiling on three sides. It looked to Piffels as if the entire elf world was here, as every seat was filled. It reminded him of the humankind sporting arenas that Master Evergreen had shown him in the forbidden books about the humankind world. A raised platform was installed on the remaining wall of the arena-like chamber. Five large throne-like chairs were arranged on the platform. He and Master Evergreen stood alone in the center of the chamber. Piffels had to fight the urge to run away from all this. Master Evergreen sensed his apprehension and placed his hand on his shoulder and whispered, "Steady on, Piffels, you will make history this day. Always remember you are not alone."

Piffels reached up to touch the hand of his Master Daemon. He thought to himself, "If I am to make history, then let it be said that no elf stood taller than Piffels Rose Blossom does on this day." He felt a warm courage rise within him. He squared his shoulders, took a deep breath, and looked up at Master Evergreen and said, "So shall it be!"

Just then trumpets sounded and four gray-haired elves, carrying long staffs, and dressed in red, blue, green and yellow robes walked into the room and climbed the stairs on the raised platform to be seated in the throne-like chairs. One chair remained empty. From the right-hand side of the room walked in the Master, dressed in a black robe and followed by a group of his followers. The Master seated himself in the fifth chair on the platform. His followers dispersed themselves into the crowd. Piffels shuddered in revulsion on seeing the Master as one of the Council of the Elder Elves.

The Elder Elf dressed in the red robe arose from his seat and pounded his staff on the platform. The sounded reverberated throughout the chamber. The huge crowd in the chamber fell silent. He spoke, "Master Elron Evergreen of Greenbrier and Piffels Rose Blossom of Greenbrier, you have been charged with treason against the land of the elves. How say you?"

"We plead not guilty to all charges," said Master Evergreen. He continued, "Who is it that brings such grievous charges against such noble elves as we?"

The Master arose from his seat, struck the bottom of his staff on the platform and said, "I, the Master, bring these charges." A murmur of voices circulated throughout the galleries of seated elves.

The Elder Elf dressed in red struck the bottom of his staff on the platform and shouted, "SILENCE!" He continued, "These are most serious charges, Master. How say you?"

The Master strode toward the front of the raised platform and raised his arms to address the crowd. As the Master looked over at them, Piffels saw what looked like a sickeningly evil grin on his face that made Piffels' body shake with revulsion.

"My friends," said the Master with his arms upraised. "Centuries ago humankind committed the most vile treachery toward the elf race. Ever since that time, we as a race have secreted ourselves away so we could live in peace. However, now that peace has been violated. Our sacred elfin lands have been …invaded by round ear humankind."

Angry shouts erupted from the crowd and the Elder Elf dressed in red had to strike his staff on the platform three times to get the crowd to quiet down.

The Master continued. "Because of the reckless behavior of the Daemons, a channel has been opened between our sacred world and the profane world of humankind. In fact, just recently, two humankind have been walking among us and spying on our ways to chart our weaknesses. I have seen this humankind with my own eyes! I fear an invasion from the humankind world is only a matter of time."

The crowd again erupted with angry shouts, and again the Elder elf in red had to strike his staff on the platform three times to get the crowd to be silent.

The Master continued, "I propose that the institution of the Daemons be disbanded and this channel between our world and the world of the humankind be forever sealed!"

There was stunned silence from the crowd. To propose disbanding the Daemons on which the villages depended was a radical proposal. It was no secret in elfin society that the Master had long desired the power of the Daemons for himself. But to hear the Master say as much in open council was unheard of.

Master Evergreen whispered in Piffels ear, "The Master's greed has just formed the rope that will bind and destroy him. Follow my lead, my son. What we say next will seal our destiny forever. Stand tall, stand tall."

The Elder Elf dressed in green arose from his chair and said, "Master Evergreen of Greenbrier, we have heard from your accuser. How say you in your defense?"

An eerie silence filled the council chamber as Master Evergreen spoke. "The Master has spoken of the ancient conflict between our elfin world and the world of humankind, but there is also an ancient prophecy, the Lattra Kree, that tells of a young elf that will seal the rift between the worlds. For too long our elfin world has languished in the backwaters of history while the world of humankind has advanced. I say it is time that we elves take our rightful place alongside our humankind brothers."

A murmur of voices rippled through the crowd as Master Evergreen continued, "No one amongst us has ventured outside the protective shield and has returned to tell the tale. That is, no one has until now! This young elf standing next to me has reached out the hand of friendship and love to the humankind world; he has ventured forth into that world and has returned to tell the tale!"

The crowd erupted in a confused mix of angry shouts and shouts of adulation and praise. Again the Elder Elf in red had to use his staff to silence the crowd.

"Piffels Rose Blossom of Greenbrier, are you the elf of which Master Evergreen of Greenbrier speaks?" asked the Elder Elf dressed in red.

Piffels stood tall and said, "I am that elf, your high honor." Again a murmur of voices rippled through the crowd.

"You, Piffels Rose Blossom of Greenbrier above all, bear the most responsibility in this matter. What say you in your defense?"

Piffels turned to face the assembled crowd of elves, paused for a moment to collect his thoughts, and then said, "I above all else desired friendship with a young humankind female named Esmeralda of Lollybump Drive. In my duties as Daemon in training, I have the opportunity to look through the Fairy Glamour Shield to observe the humankind world. I discovered that humankind are not all that different from elf kind. They may look a bit different, but if they are cut, they bleed just as we do; if they are happy they laugh and if they are sad they cry, just as we do. Just like we elves, they must drink and eat to survive, and they drink beverages and eat foods that are much the same as ours. My observations tell me that humankind and elf are brothers and sisters. I made contact to better understand and know humankind. I understand the gravity of violating sacred elfin law. However, humankind have much that can make our lives better and there is much that we can share with humankind."

A murmur of voices again rippled through the crowd. Piffels waited for the voices to subside and then continued, "Unlike the Master, I have found no malice in the hearts of humankind. I have found only love, kindness, and a sincere desire to learn about our ways. I have found no desire to invade our lands as claimed by some in our world." He paused for a moment and then continued, "I, Piffels Rose Blossom of Greenbrier, propose that it is time that we elves begin to reunite with our humankind brothers and sisters. I volunteer to brave what dangers I may face to make this so."

The crowd erupted in a confusion of voices - some voices in support and some in opposition. The Elder Elf dressed in red struck the bottom of his staff on the platform three times to silence the crowd.

Master Evergreen addressed the Elder Elves, "The Master speaks of an invasion. There is no invasion, only a desire to know, learn and understand. There are those in the humankind world who also desire reunion with their elfin brothers and sisters. Let me introduce two such brave humankind. I present ambassadors from the humankind world, Beverly and Esmeralda of Lollybump Drive."

Grandmother Beverly and Esmeralda appeared dressed in their hooded cloaks with the hoods pulled up over their heads. As they stood next to Master Evergreen and Piffels, they both removed the hoods from their heads, revealing their humankind features. A collective gasp went up from the assembled crowd.

The immense size of the chamber and the huge crowd of elves overwhelmed Esmeralda. She clung to her grandmother's side. She looked wistfully at Piffels, and he reached out to take her hand in his. At that moment Esmeralda knew that everything was going to be all right.

The Master arose from chair and angrily said, "This is a travesty and an outrage! These two are but the advance party of the humankind invasion!"

The Elder Elf dressed in red arose and said, "That is enough. You will be silent or you will leave this chamber!"

The Master just stood for a moment in stunned silence, and then said, "I as a member of the Elder Elves will not be spoken to like this! I …" The Elder Elf in red cut him off in mid sentence, "You will sit down and be silent or you will leave this chamber!"

The Master stood still for a moment and then said, "You have not heard the last from me!" Then he turned and walked out of the chamber.

A murmur of voices again circulated throughout the crowd and then faded into silence.

The Elder Elf dressed in red looked at Master Evergreen and said, "Can the worthy ambassadors from the humankind world speak on their own behalf?"

"Your high honor, they have been given the gift of elfin language," said Master Evergreen.

The Elder Elf dressed in blue looked directly at Grandmother Beverly and said, "As the elder representative of your humankind world, what say you?"

Grandmother Beverly moved to the center of the chamber, faced the Elder Elves, and said, "Your high honor, we come to your elfin world in peace and love. We desire only to know your ways and share some of our humankind world with you. Your elfin culture is one of beauty and simplicity, and we have no desire to intrude our ways on you. Young Piffels Rose Blossom of Greenbrier has risked much to try and bridge the gap between our worlds, and we honor him for this."

The Elder Elf dressed in blue looked directly at Esmeralda and said, "What say you, Esmeralda of Lollybump Drive, concerning the issue before us?"

Esmeralda looked up at her grandmother with a scared look in her eyes.

"Just speak of what is truly in your heart," Grandmother Beverly whispered in her ear.

Esmeralda stood straight and tall and then turned to face the crowd seated in the chamber. She paused for a moment and then said, "Piffels is my best friend. He is the most kind, loving and caring person I know. I love your world and the wonderful, loving and caring elves. I only wish to learn and know your ways and to share some of my own world."

Piffels moved to stand next to Esmeralda. He put his arm around her waist and Esmeralda put her head on his shoulder. A gentle murmur of voices rippled through the crowd and then all was silent.

All four of the Elder Elves grouped together in a tight circle and conferred amongst themselves. Then the Elder Elf dressed in red walked to the end of the raised platform and said, "We have come to a decision in the matter of Master Evergreen of Greenbrier and Piffels Rose Blossom of Greenbrier. We find that you, Master Evergreen, and you, Piffels, did violate the sacred law of the elves. But we also find that this violation was for the higher good of all. Therefore, the charges of high treason are found to be without merit and all such charges are dismissed."

Piffels felt a sense of relief, as if a huge weight had just been lifted from his shoulders. Master Evergreen looked down at Piffels, smiled and whispered in his ear that the best was yet to come. Piffels was not sure what Master Evergreen meant by the best yet to come, but he could feel a sense of excitement and anticipation build inside him.

A roaring crescendo of applause and cheers rang out from the crowd in the chamber. The Elder Elf dressed in yellow arose from his chair, walked to the end of the raised platform, and struck the bottom of his staff three times against the platform. The crowd in the chamber quickly grew quiet. He turned to face Master Evergreen and Piffels and said in a loud booming voice, "Master Evergreen of Greenbrier, has young Piffels Rose Blossom learned all he needs to be a Daemon?"

"Your high honor, he has mastered all the knowledge and has demonstrated the wisdom and bravery that are the hallmarks of a Daemon," said Master Evergreen with pride in his voice.

"Piffels Rose Blossom of Greenbrier, come forward," commanded the Elder Elf dressed in red. Piffels felt like he was living in a dream. As he walked toward the raised platform, he had a very strong feeling deep inside that his life was about to dramatically change forever. As Piffels walked up to the edge of the raised platform, all four of the Elder Elves also walked to the edge of the platform. The Elder Elf dressed in red said, "Kneel, Piffels." He knelt on one knee and bowed his head. The Elder Elf then lowered his staff and laid the tip of it on Piffels' left shoulder, saying, "By the power invested in us, the Council of the Elder Elves, we bestow upon you, Piffels Rose Blossom, a new name and the honor, responsibility and privileges of the Daemon. Arise, Master Braveheart Rose Blossom, Daemon of Greenbrier, and stand tall in service to your people."

Again a roar of shouts and applause rang out from the crowd in the Council chamber. Piffels heard none of it as the words of the Elder Elf rang in his mind. He stood before the Elder Elves in stunned silence.

The Elder Elf dressed in green then said, "As Daemon, one of your tasks is to serve as the first elfin ambassador to the humankind world. You shall go where no elf has gone before. We expect to hear regular reports of your adventures, and may Gaia guide your way."

Master Braveheart Rose Blossom looked up at the elder elves with tears of emotion streaming down his cheeks. "I will do my best to bring honor to our people … thank you," he said, his voice trailing off with the emotion of the moment.

The Elder Elf dressed in red raised his staff and struck the bottom on the platform three times and said, "These proceedings of the Council of the Elder Elves are closed; Gaia be praised." A chorus of cheers arose from the crowd in the Council Chamber.

Master Evergreen embraced Piffels with a big hug, and then Esmeralda wrapped her arms around him with a big hug and kissed him on the cheek. She whispered in his ear that she was so proud of him. The floor of the Council Chamber was now filled with friends and family all offering their congratulations. Piffels felt it was the happiest day of his life. And so it was, that at only thirteen years old, Piffels the little elf became the youngest Daemon in all of elfin history.

Chapter Twelve

His Name Is Piffels

This morning was colder than usual in the observatory on top of Gobstop hill as Piffels set about cleaning and arranging instruments. It was still hard for him to think of himself as the Daemon Master Braveheart. Master Evergreen had told him that in time he would grow into the new name. Very soon the new Daemon in training would be arriving to take his place with Master Evergreen. Piffels stood in the center of the observatory as warm memories of years past washed over him. One last time he swung the great seeing glass around and brought into focus the humankind world that would soon be his second home. He found himself wondering about the adventures that he knew were waiting for him in that other world. He saw his dear friend Esmeralda in the window of her house on Lollybump Drive, and a warm loving feeling filled his heart. He stepped down from the instrument and closed the observatory for the last time. It was a bittersweet moment for him as he walked down the hill to Master Evergreen's house.

"Master Braveheart, I want to introduce you to Dwingles, the new apprentice," said Master Evergreen as Piffels walked in the front door. Standing before him was a small, gangly elf wearing a shy smile. Dwingles grasped his hands in elfin greeting and said, "I have heard so much about the great Master Braveheart."

Piffels blushed, rolled his eyes, and looked over to Master Evergreen who was doing his best not to chuckle at the awkwardness Piffels felt. Piffels smiled at Dwingles and said, "It was not so long ago when I stood as you do now. I wish you well, Dwingles; you have the very best teacher in the land of the elves."

"Well now, I am hungry, let us all sit down to a wonderful morning meal," said Master Evergreen. And so it was that Master Braveheart Rose Blossom, Daemon of Greenbrier, spent his last few hours in the land of the elves.

ooooo

Communication had been established with Beverly and Esmeralda in the humankind world and they knew that in just a few moments he would be traveling as no elf had ever done. Piffels, as he still preferred his friends to call him, was lost in his own thoughts as he walked down the stone path with Master Evergreen and Dwingles to the clearing in the back garden of Master Evergreen's home. There in the center of the clearing was the silver gazing ball on a white pedestal.

"Are you ready, my son?" asked Master Evergreen.

"I am ready," said Piffels as he placed his hands on the silver gazing ball. He was desperately trying to remain calm, but his heart was racing and he felt giddy with the excitement of the moment.

Master Evergreen placed his hands on the gazing ball and intoned the words:

"Forces of the universe, I, Elron Evergreen

an elf true, send this noble elf

on a journey of discovery and adventure."

Then a pillar of sparkling light began to form around Piffels as he intoned the words:

"Hurly Burly Wackity Wee

It is off to my new home for me

May I travel in love and my

Adventures be true. Two worlds

My home will be, so shall it be."

The pillar of sparkling light grew brighter and brighter until Piffels became part of the light. A brilliant beam of light shot straight up into the sky as Piffels disappeared into the light, and his clothing crumpled to the ground. Then the light was gone and Master Evergreen and Dwingles were alone in the clearing. Master Evergreen carefully gathered up the clothing and lovingly folded it into a small box.

"He will return, Dwingles, he will return," said Master Evergreen as they both walked up the stone path to the house.

'Travel well my son, travel well,' thought Master Evergreen to himself.

ooooo

Piffels felt a tickling, tingling sensation on his skin, the sound of tinkling bells and a bright white light all around him. He felt a strong sensation of falling, falling …then the light began to fade and the image of trees, plants and blue sky began to appear. Suddenly the light was gone and he was standing in a small clearing within a garden. He felt dizzy, and the sensation of smell and sound was almost overwhelming. He could hear winged creatures singing and smell the strong organic scent of the garden and the sweet scent of flowers. It was an odd feeling, seeing flowers looking so small. Then he realized that he now was the size of humankind! He felt a chill on his skin and realized he was naked. He felt a warm cloak being placed over his shoulders, and there were Grandmother Beverly and Esmeralda.

"Steady, Piffels, the dizzy feeling will pass … it is good to see you," said Grandmother Beverly.

Esmeralda gave him a hug and said, "I am so happy you are all right."

"The sun, it is so bright! And the sounds … winged creatures, insects … so beautiful. It feels so different here," said Piffels.

"Come with us. We have some clothes for you to wear," said Grandmother Beverly. She took him by the hand and they walked up the stone path to the house.

It was amazing to Piffels to see the sea of grass in the backyard that looked so different from the standpoint of humankind size. He remembered fighting his way through the sharp blades as the furry beasts chased him, not such a long time ago. The blades of grass looked so tiny now. Every step in this new humankind world was a new discovery for him.

All three entered a back door of the house and went into small room where humankind clothing had been laid out. Piffels found the clothing was much different from his elfin clothing. The leather shoes with laces and foot dressings that Esmeralda called socks were particularly fascinating to him. Esmeralda showed him how to tighten the laces and then tie the laces at the top of the shoe. How different these were from the slip-on mouse leather shoes of his elfin world. He thought to himself what wonders he would discover in the days to come.

"Wait here in this room. We will come for you in a few moments," said Grandmother Beverly.

Esmeralda and Grandmother Beverly walked out into the kitchen. Esmeralda's mother Jane was preparing breakfast. She looked up and said, "Well, good morning you two, where have you been?"

"Oh, just enjoying the garden this morning," said Esmeralda. "Um …Mother … There is someone we would like you to meet. His name is Piffels."

And so the adventures in the humankind world began for Piffels the elf - but that is another story.

Afterword

Do you have a back garden? If not, perhaps you can set aside a small space to plant some flowers and erect a small stone wall around it. The Elfin realms exist everywhere. If you tend your garden well and leave a small area amongst the flowers, mosses and colored stones, you just never know where the elves may decide to build a village.

When Master Evergreen was asked the question, "So where in the humankind world are the elves and fairies?" He just smiled and said, "Why, we are everywhere. A forest glade there, a garden plot here, you just never know exactly where."

Would this world not be a better place if we set aside some places to plant beautiful flowers and to invite the elves and fairies to share this world with us? And perhaps some day you may find a little hand written note on your dressing table that says, "Hello, I am an elf and I want to be your friend."

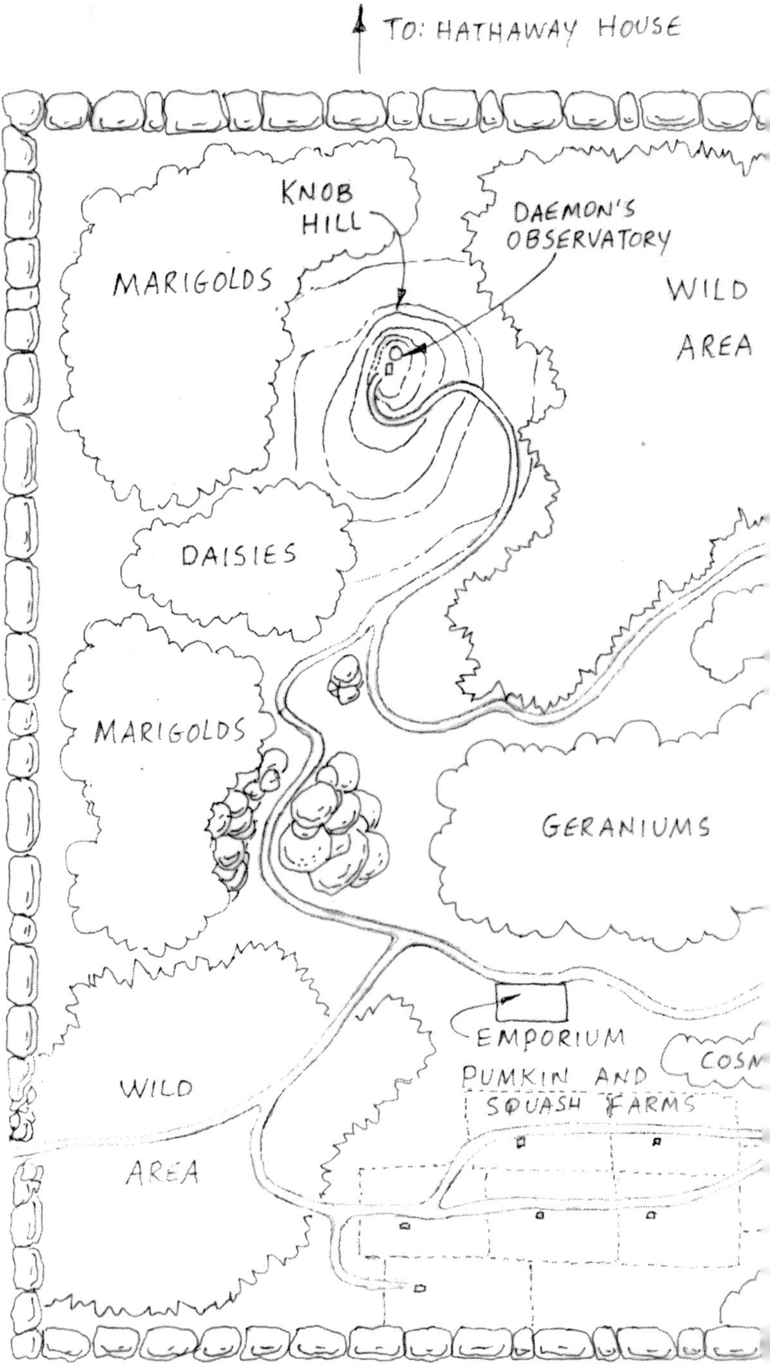

TO: HATHAWAY HOUSE

KNOB HILL

DAEMON'S OBSERVATORY

MARIGOLDS

WILD AREA

DAISIES

MARIGOLDS

GERANIUMS

EMPORIUM

COSM

WILD

AREA

PUMKIN AND SQUASH FARMS

Elfin Realm

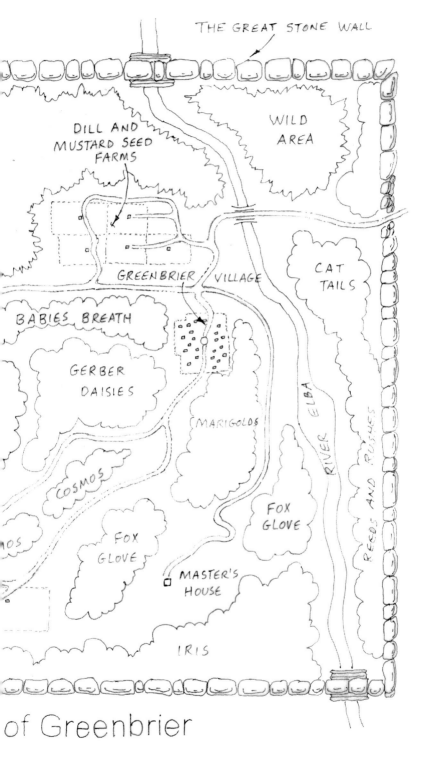

THE GREAT STONE WALL

WILD AREA

DILL AND MUSTARD SEED FARMS

GREENBRIER VILLAGE

CAT TAILS

BABIES BREATH

GERBER DAISIES

MARIGOLDS

COSMOS

RIVER ELBA

REEDS AND RUSHES

FOX GLOVE

OS

FOX GLOVE

FOX GLOVE

MASTER'S HOUSE

IRIS

of Greenbrier

The Author

Dr. David Babulski is the author of over sixty technical publications in the disciplines of physics, electronics, aeronautics, mineralogy and astronomy. He holds a Baccalaureate degree in Earth Science and Masters and Doctoral degrees in Science Education. He also holds a diploma from the Institute for Children's Literature and he is an award winning mineral artist. Professionally he is a technical educator with over thirty-four years of experience.

In his spare time, he is writing several books, plays the Celtic harp and is active in model aeronautics, mineral art, amateur radio, astronomy and is a student of metaphysics.

Other Books Available from Andborough Publishing

Children's Reiki Handbook, 2nd Edition

ISBN : 978-0-9774181-5-2
paperback

Only $17.95

**Amazon.com and
Barnes&Noble.com
Energy Healing Bestseller**

Reiki is an Japanese system of energy healing through the "laying on of hands" that is simple enough for children of all ages to learn.

The Children's Reiki Handbook is a guide to energy healing that provides kids with the information they need to prepare for their First, Second and Master Reiki Attunement; and shows them how to use their new skills to heal themselves and others.

"I found Children's Reiki Handbook to be a concise yet thorough introduction to the Usui healing system of Reiki. It's perfect for children and young adults"
- ML Rhodes, Amazon #1 Best Selling Author
and Usui Reiki Ryoho Master/Teacher

"If you want to learn Reiki, this book will serve as in inspiration towards that goal... This Reiki handbook is a great resource to introduce the benefits of Reiki healing to children or grown ups who are just starting out."
- Erin Kelly-Allshouse, Review Editor
Children of the New Earth

Temple of the Twelve
Novice of Colors

ISBN-13: 978-0-9774181-8-3

278 pages paperback

$17.95

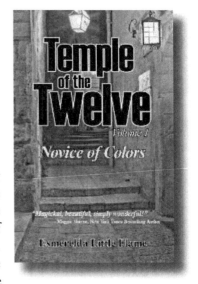

The sixteen year old daughter of a poor woodcutter, Caroline was born into a world where the Twelve were said to be the stuff of legends and children's stories.

She had always known the truth – that the Twelve were very real and living amongst humankind even now. But when she ended up at their Temple she didn't quite believe it was real herself.

Still, when the Twelve began to appear to her in human form – when they began to teach her their lessons – they changed everything in her life. She began to understand that it was her destiny to be a bridge between the past and the future in a world that was changing too fast.

She formed bonds with an ancient clan who kept the ways of the Twelve alive, in hiding and seclusion. Her love for the Twelve deepened into unconditional loving devotion – It was a love that would take her from girlhood into the soul of a young woman.

For love of the Twelve, Caroline began to understand, she would do anything... Anything at all.

....

"Magickal, beautiful, simply wonderful!"
> - Maggie Shayne, New York Times Bestselling Author

"...prose is music to the mind...weaves a whimsical tapestry of warmth and delight..."
> - Silver Ravenwolf, Bestselling Author of *Teen Witch* and *Solitary Witch*

Dream of the
Circle of Women

ISBN-13: 978-0-9774181-9-0

330 pages paperback

$17.95

Soon after arriving at the house she's just inherited from the birth mother she never met, Kat begins to have a series of vivid recurring dreams about a group of women who drown themselves in the sea rather than be persecuted as witches.

As she learns about her new home and her birth mother, Kat finds herself with more and more questions, discovers hidden secrets in the centuries old house, and uncovers a disturbing truth of her lineage.   But will she find the answers she needs before tragedy strikes her?

....

What others are saying about
Dream of the Circle of Women...

"...Blanchard manages to completely enrapture the reader...Dream [of the Circle of Women] is a masterpiece for readers of any age group. Well done, and more...please!"

– Shelley Glodowski, Senior
Reviewer Midwest Book Review

"This is by far one of the best pagan fiction books I have found. Dream of the Circle of Women is imaginative, engaging, and inspiring."

– Jennifer Erwin,
Facing North Book Reviews

Printed in the United States
140499LV00001B/4/P

9 780982 397107